The Truth

Book Three in The Descendant Vampire Series

Kelley Grealis

The Truth
Copyright ©2014 KG Publishing, LLC

Cover design by Rick Kundrach for Icandi Graphics
Edited by Jenny Bengen-Albert

ISBN-13: 978-1499108095
ISBN-10: 1499108095

Praise for The Descendant, Book 1 in The Descendant Vampire Series

"*The Descendant* is a unique paranormal tale that takes a well known Biblical theme and turns it sideways, resulting in a thoughtful, well written story of one woman's discovery of a family legacy that changes both her perception of her past and her expectations of her future."

  —Gigi Siguenza, Indie Love Book Club

"I look forward to other stories Grealis may pen in non-vampire settings because, in all honesty, she has a vision and way of telling a story few authors possess. After all, if she could get a die-hard anti-vampire reader like me interested in her characters enough to want to read the sequel, *The Search* —to be released later in 2013, I'd say she did a commendable job indeed."

  —Budden Book Reviews

"The story that Kelley Grealis weaved in *The Descendant* was so freaking creative that my mouth dropped a few times. I was happy, I was scared, I even cried before the first half of the book was over, and she delivered an emotional roller coaster that in my book deserves 5 Stars in high-def! I can't wait for more from this author to see what is next. I loved it!"

  —AJ Lape, author of the Darcy Walker Series

"Kelley Grealis successfully had me crying before I made it to chapter four, and pissed by chapter nine as I started to figure things out. This really was a roller coaster of a book that struck a nerve on so many amazing levels. As for the ending —you know I am a stickler for an ending —Kelley Grealis did me proud! She successfully gave me an ending that left me feeling fulfilled with a clear conclusion, while leaving a crack of an opening for more. Bravo!"

—Bex 'N' Books, Book Reviewer & Blogger

"Ms. Grealis demonstrates the necessary prerequisite of a popular author: a knack for telling an engaging story. Nothing else really matters if that isn't the underpinning."

—Smidhja, Amazon Reviewer

"This book is, for a lack of a better word, AMAZING! I love the spin on the Biblical story. So original! It also brought out so many emotions! Sorrow, angst, anger, good, old-fashioned swooning, I experienced it all with Allison. I know I'll be adding this to my 'To be read again' pile."

—J.D. Nelson, Author of Night Aberrations and A Night of Wickedness

"Grealis proves herself an accomplished storyteller in this vampire thriller. I am not the greatest fan of the genre as it is all too easy to fall into the clichéd traps. However Grealis gamely avoids garlic and conveniently sunny windows to put her own stamp on things. Her take on the origins of vampires is one I have never seen before and makes for an interesting read. The writing is fantastic and she manages to draw you in and trap you within her pages until she has had her fill of you."

—Gray, Amazon Reviewer

Praise for The Search, Book 2 in The Descendant Vampire Series

"The uniqueness of these vampire books is a huge A+! I love the Biblical weave she brings into every tale, giving you more nuggets that make you wonder if maybe vampires are real!"

—Natasha House, Author & Amazon Reviewer

"Kelley Grealis takes her characters through more twists and turns to drive the reader into a frenzy of excitement bringing you to care for those who are to remain damned for eternity."

—Angela Crandall, Amazon Reviewer

"This is no ordinary vampire story."

—Carmen Reyes, Amazon Reviewer

"I thought I was hooked with book 1, I think it's safe to say this book made it an addiction."

—The Pink Bookshelf

"Kelley Grealis' method of storytelling is refreshing and clever. Very well thought out and engaging."

—Cynthia, Amazon Reviewer

"This author has a way to keep you engaged in the story and wanting more of what is to come next."

—Autumn Nauling for Fallen Over Book Reviews

"As much as I enjoyed the first book in this series, this second book has cemented Grealis as an author I plan to watch."

—Joyce Wetherbee, Amazon Reviewer

"I LOVED this vampire series. This is the best one that I've read."

—Jenjen0130, Amazon Reviewer

"I would give this more than 5 stars if I could. You simply MUST read it!!"

—Dowie, Amazon Reviewer

"Didn't know it was possible, but better than the first!!"

—I Feel the Need, the Need to Read, Blogger & Amazon Reviewer

Table of Contents

Dedication

To all those who seek the truth, may you find it.

Chapter 1

Something was amiss. I noticed it immediately as I withdrew from my meditative state and regained control of my senses. It wasn't the tingling sensation in my legs from having hung upside down as I rested all night. It wasn't the individual specks coalescing to form the full view of my living room below. It wasn't the sound of chirping crickets I heard beyond the walls of my home, or the sting of hunger on my tongue or the ravenous void in my belly. None of that was what was wrong. It was the scent assaulting my nostrils. It was more than just *his* scent left on me from last evening's escapade. His scent was stronger, heavier, hanging in the air like recently sprayed cologne. That meant one thing – he was close, he was here. And he wasn't supposed to be here.

"Get out," I growled.

I glared down at the wood floor, not daring to look over at him for fear of my reaction upon actually laying eyes on him. I didn't need to see him to confirm he was here. My vampire senses had alerted me to his presence and the fact he had ignored my wishes last night when I had told him to leave and that was enough to incite me.

I straightened my legs, the movement causing me to fall from the ceiling beam I had been using as a meditation perch. A half summersault later and I was on my feet staring up at *him*.

Deep breaths did little to calm me. Anger rose in me like mercury in a thermometer on a hot summer's day. My ears burned with rage. I fisted both hands, nails gouging flesh, and clenched my jaw. Couldn't he feel my gaze boring a hole through him?

"Get out," I shouted. My voice ricocheted off of the walls and echoed throughout the Ridge Hollow forest surrounding my home. Birds took flight as my demand reverberated through the treetops. But yelling didn't faze him. He remained perfectly still. I knew better. Neither staring nor shouting would wake a resting vampire.

The warm trail of blood on my hands diverted my attention. I relaxed my fingers and my nails withdrew from my flesh. I stared at my palms and watched the wounds heal like they had never been there, then shifted my eyes to the couch. Surveying the plethora of throw pillows, I picked up one after the other and heaved them with increasing strength in his direction. "Get out, get out, get out, God damn it, GET OUT!"

Pillow number three drilled Vincent squarely in the chest, and my message finally registered. He defensively waved his arms as he woke from his slumber. I continued throwing pillows as he fell to the floor where he landed cat-like on both feet.

"Well good morning to you," Vincent said as he straightened his black button down shirt. His deep, smooth voice, something that once made my heart flutter, was now akin to the teeth-gritting sound of nails scratching a chalkboard.

My gaze wandered to the patch of skin exposed as a result of his sheer laziness in neglecting to button the top four buttons of his shirt. As he moved, I could see the crease between his well-defined pecs. A vision from last night flashed across my mind… my hand caressing that bare chest as we lay in bed, his hand massaging the small of my back. I cut off the thought before my mind recalled what had happened next. One look at his face was all I needed to confirm it was more than laziness that had caused him to "forget" to button his shirt. He smiled, his come-hither eyes twinkling. I wasn't going to fall for it.

"Get out," I said through gritted teeth.

His smile widened as he realized the effect he was having on me. He was pushing all of my buttons in the way he alone knew how. A combination of lust and hate coursed through me. I was appalled with myself for allowing one man to make me feel such a roller coaster of emotions.

"I heard you the third time, dear. Did you wake up on the wrong side of the bed?" Vincent walked into the kitchen, and even though the open floor plan allowed me to see him from the living room, I was compelled to follow him.

"I told you last night to leave. I don't want you spending the night here. We are not a couple, damn it."

"Oh come on, Allison." Vincent stopped in the middle of the kitchen and turned to face me. "You keep saying we're not a couple, but your actions say otherwise."

His crystal blue eyes bore into mine, and I felt violated as he tried to search my soul. The intimacy of the moment produced another memory from last night—him rolling on top and pinning me underneath his body. Soft kisses caressing my neck as his fingers danced across my body as if it were his personal dance floor. And me enjoying every time his body touched mine and the sheer need and desire that contact produced. I squeezed my eyes shut, hoping that would allow me to forget what I had once again done after vowing several times I'd never do it again.

"I don't know why you just can't admit it so we can move past this... well, whatever this is," he said as he waved a hand in my direction.

"We... are not... a couple," I hissed as I struggled to suppress the creator's bond and what it was doing to me.

"Come now, dear," Vincent said. He wrapped an arm around my waist and turned my face toward him with his other hand. "We spent the spring traveling to Paris, Monaco, the Canary Islands and Greece. You remember the daytimes filled with handholding and sightseeing, don't you? And the moonlit dinners? And then of course," Vincent pressed his body to mine and leaned into my ear to whisper, "there were the passion fueled nights where we showed each other exactly what we meant to each other. I'd say we're a couple."

I groaned and pushed him away. "I somewhat remember what you're talking about. But wait, that feels like it was so long ago and, oh yeah, the trip was cut short when you tricked me into returning to Castle Adena. Things get a little fuzzy after that. Remember why?"

Vincent winced. "Allison, I had to."

"You said you could help me control my urge for human blood. At least that's the line you fed me before you convinced me to run off and see all of the places I'd always wanted to see. You lied."

"Do you think I wanted to lie to you? What can I say? Max was right. I should have listened to my brother sooner. You needed help. I couldn't see how bad your addiction was. I thought I could have helped you."

"Oh! So are you actually admitting you were wrong about something? Newsflash! Vincent Drake admits he was wrong."

"Allison, how many times do I have to apologize? You needed help and you weren't going to go willingly. Max and I did what was necessary to ensure you got the help you needed. And look at you now. Your urges are under control. Isn't that all that matters? I don't understand why we can't resume our trip so I can take you to other places you dreamed of seeing. You were so happy and carefree and, dare I say, in love. That's how you seemed to me, and I want to see that side of you again."

I bit my lower lip and drew blood. Turning around, I washed the dried blood off my hands before leaning on the countertop and dropping my head. *You're a rebound*, I thought. I desperately wanted to utter those words but feared Vincent's reaction.

After everything that had happened this past March–discovering Matt, my husband of seven years, was an archangel in Saint Michael's Army, and we couldn't be together because an angel/vampire affair would have supposedly set off a war between the enemy factions–I had turned to Vincent for comfort. Initially, I had let the creator's bond get the better of me and it had everything to do with the way I felt toward Vincent. The bond between the creator and the vampire he or she creates never goes away, but allow the bond to get the better of you, and you're suddenly blinded by a love that doesn't exist. I was overcome with loyalty toward my creator and used that to mask the pain of losing Matt. Loyalty turned into infatuation and the illusion of love.

After regaining control of my need for human blood, other urges had become more pronounced, namely the need for physical contact. I was sure Vincent knew that would be a side effect of my detox and was more than happy to fulfill my needs. But the better I got at controlling my need for human blood, the better I got at controlling other needs, too. I was able to reign in the creator's bond and realized what I was doing, or rather what I was allowing to happen. And I didn't like it. Not that I didn't like sex with Vincent, because the sex was mind-blowingly fantastic; I didn't like whom I was doing it with. With sobriety came clarity and with clarity came reality. And reality was I was in love. With Matt, my husband. I no longer hated Vincent for having transformed me into a vampire. I had consented, as I'd learned earlier this year, and that was on me. I now hated Vincent because he simply wasn't Matt. Vincent filled a void. Although he filled the physical void quite well, he couldn't fill the void in my heart, an emptiness that could never be filled.

"Allison–"

"I told you I'm not ready for the next step." I turned around. "I'm not ready for a committed relationship. It's too soon."

Vincent raised his thumb to my mouth and wiped away the blood. He leaned in and gently licked where I had bitten my lip. His venom tingled as it healed my flesh. He pulled away, not breaking eye contact. His icy blue eyes didn't make my stomach flutter. His warm hand on my cheek didn't send waves of desire throughout my body. "So are you just using me for my body?"

It took me a moment to process the comment. "You're kidding, right?"

Vincent arched an eyebrow and shrugged a shoulder.

I groaned. "You need to leave." I pushed past him and walked into the pantry, pretending to look for something.

"Lighten up, Allison. I was only joking." Vincent poked his head into the pantry.

"Seriously. Leave. I have something to do today," I lied.

"Does it have anything to do with your dream? I'd like to help you figure it out. Maybe we can drive around the city to see if we find any landmarks resembling the statue in your dreams."

I grabbed a teabag and pushed Vincent out of my way as I retrieved a coffee cup from the cupboard.

For months I'd been having the same dream. It always started the same, with me standing outside of a black wrought iron gate surrounding a shaded grassy area. Once inside the gate, I wandered, unable to see any defined shape, my vision hampered by what seemed like eyeglasses with the wrong prescription. All I could discern were shiny colored shapes scattered over the ground–some flat, others raised, all in various sizes. The only object I could see clearly was an angel statue that came to life, stomping to attract my attention and then pointing in a direction, but to what or where, I didn't know. The dream never advanced beyond that. I was initially happy Vincent had offered to help decipher the dream's meaning. But now that I was sober and my emotions were in check, his persistence was just plain annoying. In fact, his insistence bordered on suspicious.

"No, it has nothing to do with that." I walked to the fridge and filled the cup with water.

"Does this thing you have to do have anything to do with Matthew?"

My back stiffened at the sound of Matt's name. Every nerve in my body tingled as if I'd been tasered. I turned around with the cup of water and walked to the microwave, avoiding eye contact. I placed the cup on the glass tray and slammed the door. "No, Vincent, it doesn't. Now can you please leave like I asked you to?"

Vincent walked to me and grabbed my chin with one hand. I tried to break free but he wouldn't allow it. His eyes combed my face, looking for answers. "Well I can see you're in one of your moods." He released my chin, his analysis complete. "I hope whatever it is you have to do today brings a smile to your beautiful face." He leaned in and gently kissed me. Backing away slowly, he waited for a reaction, and when I didn't give him one, he left.

I expelled a breath I hadn't realized I'd been holding and reached for my cell phone. I swiped the screen to see if there were any new emails, texts or missed calls. I had plenty, but none from the one person I was hoping to hear from. There were several texts from Max, probably checking in like he did most days to ensure I hadn't fallen off the wagon, and a couple of missed calls from Marlo. I checked my sent messages and confirmed the most recent one had been delivered to Matt's phone. I then checked my outgoing calls and emails to make sure I hadn't imagined calling and emailing him.

"What in the hell, Matt," I muttered. I knew we couldn't be together. Matt had made that perfectly clear after the battle with Lucious and Jal on Rattlesnake Island this past March. He had all of the Army's talking points down, including the angel's ridiculous rules about angels and vampires not interacting, because doing so would set off a war between the age-old enemies. On one hand, you had the Devil's creation–vampires, me included–whose sole purpose was to kill mortals and damn their souls for eternity. The angels, on the other hand, were an army sanctioned by God, sent to Earth to protect man from vampires. I got it. Kind of. But Matt and I were different. We had been husband and wife before we were archangel and vampire. That had to mean something, but apparently it didn't.

I had previously somehow convinced Matt to meet me for a beer at the end of July. He had been hesitant at first, playing by the angels' rules and saying he couldn't–that we couldn't. But when I told him I had cleaned up my act and gotten my hunger under control, I seemed to have piqued his interest. I had hoped he would have wanted to see me because he truly missed me, as I did him. But I think he only agreed because curiosity had gotten the better of him. Maybe he had to see with his own eyes I was no longer the uncontrollable monster he had heard about in all of the rumors about my killing spree.

When we saw each other, my heart had literally skipped a beat. I wanted to jump out of my seat and pull him to me, but he had flinched upon my approach. I had decided to take it slow and instead extended a hand for him to sit at the table. Conversation was initially difficult. We sat there and stared at our beers, failing miserably at our attempts at small talk. Matt seemed uncomfortable and on edge as he constantly shifted on his bar stool, guzzling his beer and staring out into the parking lot. His reaction was understandable given the elephant in the room; our eighth wedding anniversary had been only two days prior but had gone uncelebrated given I'd widowed Matt once I transformed. But a couple of pints later, it was like the old Matt and Ali–the two of us sitting at our favorite brew pub talking about everything and anything. Until *she* showed up.

Gabriela spoiled the party. Matt's handler ever since the car accident that landed me in the hospital with amnesia, Gabriela was there to teach Matt the way of the angel world. And that included no rendezvousing with vampires. No exceptions. She made a scene, scolded us like children and demanded Matt leave. And leave he did.

I ignored Gabriela's message and reached back out to Matt, somehow convincing him to meet me again. Maybe all of the boozing and reminiscing sparked something in him. I didn't know. All I knew was that he was game, and I couldn't have been any happier.

We hatched an elaborate plan for Matt to sneak out of his house and throw Gabriela off his trail. This was necessary as she was still taking up residence in our Buzzard Hill home. She had lived there since the accident, when Vincent had returned Matt home after the car wreck, and given our meeting at the bar, Matt suspected Gabriela was keeping a close eye on him.

Our plan was to meet at a winery in Geneva-on-the-Lake—a town far, far away from Buzzard Hill by at least ninety minutes. A place so far out of the way it wouldn't be possible to run into anyone we knew by chance. Matt texted on his way that he thought he was in the clear. I anxiously awaited his arrival, my finger circling the rim of a wine glass, my eyes glued to the winery's entrance. The door swung open, and Matt stood there bathed in sunlight as if the big man upstairs had sanctioned our visit. He took two steps forward. I stood, ready to greet him, and then froze as Gabriela walked in behind him. She compelled the bartender and other visitors out of the building and gave us a tongue lashing like no other, threatening to report our actions to the Army. She made it clear that the repercussions would definitely not be something we would want to experience.

Since then, there had been nothing. No returned phone calls, no texts, not even an email to let me know he was still alive.

"This is bullshit," I cursed. "You can't ignore me like this. What's the harm with a simple text?"

I scanned the room, not looking for anything in particular, and then my gaze settled on a picture frame on the sofa table. The black frame showcased a dried rosebud I had found pressed between waxed paper and flattened by the weight of the Bible I'd discovered it in. A light bulb went on in my head. I had the perfect excuse to go to Buzzard Hill. I grabbed my car keys and headed toward the garage. I was going to pay Matt a visit.

Chapter 2

I pulled into the driveway and killed the Corvette's engine. Taking in the sight of the mailbox post and the metal letters that spelled my last name, I took a deep breath and slowly, deliberately exhaled. My palms started to sweat, and my stomach flip-flopped. A wave of nausea swept over me as I looked at the front of the house, wondering what type of greeting I'd receive.

My gaze lingered on the house as my mind drifted back to the day Matt and I had moved in. After the movers left, I had been feeling overwhelmed with all of the boxes that needed unpacking when Matt snuck up behind me and whisked me away to the master bedroom which we promptly christened. After finding our robes, we walked through each of the three spare bedrooms and talked about the kids we wanted to have and which rooms our son and daughter would occupy. Sadly, children were never a reality for us. Plagued by years of infertility, I had recently learned the problem was with me–the problem *was* me. Female vampires couldn't conceive. Now this large house stood, half empty, like the dreams Matt and I once had.

My cell phone vibrated in my pocket. I pulled it out and saw that it was Max. His persistence this morning in wanting to connect for our daily check-in grated on my nerves. It had been over two months since I completed his version of vampire rehab. If he was so confident in his ability to break my addiction to human blood, then where was the trust?

I tapped "ignore" and tucked the phone back in the pocket of my leather pants. That conversation could wait.

I exited the car and surveyed my surroundings. The neighborhood was quiet; no one was outside enjoying the warm September day. Some things never changed. Everyone complained about being cooped up during the long, frigid Cleveland winters, yet when the nice weather finally arrived, everyone stayed cooped up in their air-conditioned homes.

Chirping crickets and the buzzing of other late summer insects filled the air as a gentle breeze ruffled leaves on the verge of giving way to their fall hues. Sunlight glinted off of the green street sign that read Peace Eagle Pass. I looked back at Matt's house, our former home together, and took another breath. Tightness stretched across my chest as anxiety began to get the better of me.

"Calm down, Allison," I whispered. "There's nothing to be afraid of."

My phone buzzed again. This time it was Marlo. As I had done with Max, I ignored the call. I assumed Max had sounded the warning bell, and now Marlo was on point as well. But she could also wait.

I walked up the driveway and noticed Jenna's car parked by the garage doors. In our first meeting, Matt had mentioned Jenna, my best friend since kindergarten, had been staying with him and Gabriela ever since the incident on Rattlesnake Island. At first, Gabriela insisted that Jenna stay for her own safety. Having witnessed the battle and discovered the existence of vampires, archangels and magic, Jenna had been exposed to centuries-old secrets no human was supposed to know. From a vampire's perspective, that knowledge would typically mean death to any mere mortal, but Gabriela announced that Jenna would become part of the flock, thereby protecting her from vampire retaliation. Harming Jenna was now the equivalent of harming an archangel and would trigger retribution from the Army. And I'd heard more than once that no vampire wanted to experience the wrath of Saint Michael's Army.

In the months since, it had been Jenna's preference to stay at my former home, stating she felt safe there. As for Gabriela, it appeared Matt couldn't get rid of her. She had settled in and felt the need to babysit him as well as Jenna. Another car, one I didn't recognize, was parked behind Jenna's.

The row of barberry bushes bordering the walkway to the front door were overdue for a trim, as was the grass whose long blades fluttered in the breeze. The unkemptness was uncharacteristic of Matt, as he had always prided himself on a well-manicured yard.

I hopped up the three steps and paused on the landing. Staring at the burnt orange door, I wondered what Matt would think of me showing up at the house unannounced. Would he be happy to see me or would he shoo me away? Would he even be home? I hadn't considered that before jumping in the Vette and speeding over here. Maybe I should have at least texted to have given him a heads up.

My phone vibrated again. It was a text from Max asking where I was and telling me to call him immediately. I stuffed the phone in my pocket. *Later, Max, later.* I raised my hand to knock when the door swung open.

"What are you doing here?" Matt whispered.

"Well nice to see you too." I scanned him from head to toe, drinking in his handsomeness. He'd added some bulk since the last time I had seen him. His white t-shirt stretched across his chest and clung to his sculpted biceps. His black tribal band tattoo peeked out from under the shirtsleeve on his left arm. My eyes circled it and then drifted down to his v-shaped midsection tucked into blue jeans that snuggly hugged muscular thighs. He cleared his throat, and I returned my attention to his face. Impeccably flawless skin, those sweet hazel eyes, three days' worth of stubble and hair a bit longer than usual, tousled like he had just gotten out of bed. It took all of the self-control I had to not pull him to me and kiss him.

"You can't be here, you know?" he said, not condescending, but as if I should have already known.

"I–"

A slender brunette jogged down the staircase. Her wavy hair fell past her shoulders. She was gathering it to pull back into a ponytail. She wasn't a vampire, but I couldn't assess whether or not she was an archangel. A short t-shirt revealed a toned midriff. A duffle bag draped over one shoulder and across her body.

"Goodbye, Matt," she said and pecked him on the cheek. "I'll call you later." She made eye contact as she walked past me and to the unfamiliar car sitting in the driveway. That mystery was answered and it also explained Matt's messy hair.

"Who was that?" I demanded. "The reason why the yard work has been neglected?" My face flushed at the thought of *that* woman in bed with Matt.

"Ali." He cocked his head as if asking me not to ask any more questions.

"Who is she?" I cracked my knuckles and then strummed my fingers against my leg.

"You know we're not married anymore."

"Is she your girlfriend? Are you dating?"

"Ali, why are you here?"

"Well if you'd answer my calls or texts or emails, maybe I wouldn't have crashed your booty call."

"What are you talking about? What calls and texts?"

"Way to avoid answering my questions about her."

"I'm not going to answer your questions about her, but I really don't know what you're talking about. What messages?"

"Oh don't play coy with me, Matt. I've sent you dozens of messages over the past month and you haven't responded to one. I've left you tons of voicemails but you don't have the courtesy to call back and let me know you're still alive. We may not be married any longer, but I still worry about you. But you seemingly haven't had so much as a thought of me, I see. Someone else obviously has your attention."

"Ali, I'm serious, I don't know what you're talking about. I haven't received any messages from you since we tried meeting at Church Vineyards."

"Mmm hmm." My phone buzzed multiple times as several texts came in. Matt glanced at my pocket and then at my face, asking without saying a word if I was going to answer them. I pursed my lips and cocked my head, waiting for his response.

"Honestly." Matt held up both hands defensively. "I thought Gabriela's speech might have sunk in with you. I know her threats struck a chord with me."

As if on cue, the sound of stilettos knocking against the hardwood floor announced Gabriela's presence. She sashayed past the entryway separating the foyer from the sunken living room, her gauzy white dress flowing behind her. Her lip curled up in a devilish grin as she acknowledged my presence.

"Ugh," I uttered. Now it all made sense.

Matt turned around. "You!" He pointed a finger at Gabriela who turned and leaned against the wall. "Have you been deleting messages from my phone?"

She raised an eyebrow and a shoulder indicating she didn't know what Matt was talking about. She giggled as she turned and walked out of sight.

"Well there you have it," Matt said.

"You're just going to let her get away with it?"

"No, I'll deal with her later. But right now, I need to know why you stopped over today, Ali-gator?" The corner of his mouth quivered, wanting to smile, but apprehension restrained all emotion.

The sound of his nickname for me rolling off his tongue sent a round of warm and fuzzy feelings all over my body. When we had first started dating, Matt noticed pretty quickly that my temper could strike without notice. He said I snapped like an alligator, and that's how the nickname came to be. Over the years, he had used it as a term of endearment. I was his Ali-gator. He'd use it in passing or use it an attempt to calm me, like he was attempting right now. And it was working. I looked down at my feet and couldn't help but smile. I didn't know who the brunette was who had just left the house, and I didn't need to know. What I was certain of was that she couldn't possibly have as meaningful a relationship as Matt and I had. After all we'd been through, especially over the past year, I think Matt still cared for me, otherwise he wouldn't have used that term of endearment. What we had, the love we had shared, couldn't be erased with one vampire/angel battle and a couple of threats from Gabriela. We had a love that could stand the test of time.

"Um," I blushed and looked back up at Matt. "I was hoping to pick up some artwork we have in the attic."

Matt tilted his head as if not understanding.

"I've, um, been thinking a lot lately about my parents. I remember my mom and I made artwork out of dried rose petals. We'd paste petals from each year's blooms onto canvas. If I recall correctly, I think we stored the piece in the attic next to the chest filled with your grandmother's handmade blankets."

"Oh, yeah. I remember. Sure, I don't think that would be a problem."

Gabriela sprung from out of nowhere. "No, Matthew."

"Excuse me?" I questioned.

"She can't have it."

"Gabriela, the artwork belongs to Ali."

"But–"

"But nothing. You were obviously eavesdropping so you had to have heard Ali. She and her mom created it. And besides, it's just sitting in the attic collecting dust."

I smirked at Gabriela. She responded with a snarl.

"I'll help you find it, Matt," I said. I took a step toward the threshold but was stopped by the invisible force preventing a vampire from entering the home of an archangel.

It was Gabriela's turn to smirk. "Seriously, Matt?"

He sighed. "That," he said, tilting his head toward the threshold, "I can't help." He tossed his head in Gabriela's direction indicating where the blame should be placed. Gabriela turned on her heels and left the living room.

I rolled my eyes. I wished I could get my hands on Gabriela and show her exactly how I felt about her. My phone vibrated again. Matt looked at my pocket.

"Sounds like someone is trying to get ahold of you."

I huffed and retrieved the phone. There were a dozen missed calls and twice as many texts from Max, Marlo and Lorenzo. "Good grief," I muttered.

"I'll um, go get the picture," Matt said. He took the steps two at a time as he bounded up to the second level where he could access the attic.

My phone rang. "What?" I barked at Max.

"Allison, where are you? I've been trying to get ahold of you all morning.""Yeah, I noticed. Between you, Marlo and Lorenzo my phone has been buzzing nonstop this morning."

"And you don't bother to answer any of our calls? Never mind," he snapped before I could interject. "You need to come to Castle Adena immediately.""You know, Max, a little trust goes a long way. I haven't strayed from my diet since leaving your rehab. My urges are under control. I even had a couple of blood bags this morning."

"It's not that. Felix is dead."

Chapter 3

Every bit of the Corvette's 505 horsepower engine was tapped to get me from Buzzard Hill to Castel Adena in record time. Once at the Drake's residence, I had no idea how I had driven there, as I didn't recall most of the trip. My mind was otherwise occupied with Felix and how he had died. Max hadn't given any details. I hadn't let him. As soon as he had uttered *Felix is dead*, I disconnected the call and sprinted to my car.

As I drove on autopilot, several scenarios about how Felix had met his demise ran through my mind. Did he find himself at the wrong place at the wrong time? Could an angel have intercepted him as he had hunted human prey? I dismissed the idea given Max's detailed hunting regimen that limited mortal kills in concentrated areas. The Drakes had avoided the angels' radar for so long it seemed unlikely an angel would have caught Felix about to kill a mortal and intervened to save the person's soul. Could Felix have possibly run into an enemy who had exacted revenge? I couldn't think of any enemies Felix might have had, but having existed for over two millennia, I was sure he had racked up an enemy or two. Vampires, after all, were a vengeful lot. Or was it something else I couldn't think of? Whatever had happened, there was one certainty: the killer knew how to kill a vampire by ripping out his throat and staking him through the stomach, stopping the source of the Devil's evilness that propelled every vampire's existence. The thought of that happening to Felix made my stomach lurch.

I shoved the shifter into neutral, yanked the emergency brake and shut off the engine before the car was fully stopped. I hopped out, slamming the door shut as I ran to the castle's entrance. It didn't even dawn on me that the door was open. I entered the foyer and yelled, "Hello." There was no answer. "Max, I'm here," I yelled again.

"Allison, I presume?"

I whirled around and saw a man. He wore a black suit and white shirt, so I assumed he was a butler, one of many the Drakes had on staff. His long brown hair was slicked back into a ponytail, and hazel eyes glinted in the sunlight. He quickly stepped out of the ray filtering through the window.

"Makes your blood boil, you know?" he quipped.

"Yeah, I'm familiar," I cautiously responded.

A closer look at his eyes revealed thirteen gold flecks, the telltale sign of a vampire. My mind flipped through a catalog of faces I'd seen during the time I was held captive here while in rehab, but his face was unfamiliar. "Who are you?" I demanded.

"Pardon me," the man said as he bowed. "I'm one of the Drake's butlers. Please follow me upstairs where you may wait until the Drakes are ready for you."

The man walked past me and through the doorway leading to the staircase to the second level. I eyed him suspiciously as I hadn't recalled seeing him in the past. Then again, I couldn't possibly keep track of the entire staff; there were butlers, maids, gardeners and a plethora of other workers who kept the castle and grounds in order. And given the condition I had been in as I detoxed, I may have missed a few details. I attributed my suspicions to recent events–Felix's death.

"Are you coming?" He leaned around the doorway and raised an eyebrow.

"Um, yeah."

"You can wait in the blue room," he said as we ascended the staircase. "It's my understanding you've stayed in that room before. Some of the décor has been updated and I hope you find the changes pleasing. But some décor remains unchanged. The ocean painting you were fond of is still hanging on the wall."

"What?" I questioned. Mention of the painting caught me off guard. Sure I remembered the room; it was where I had completed my transformation into a vampire. I woke in that room a changed woman, no longer a mortal, but a monster created in the Devil's own likeness. How did this man know anything about my transformation, let alone any supposed affinity I had toward the painting? But the butler ignored my question and continued on.

"The Drakes should be with you shortly." He opened the door and ushered me in.

"Where are they?"

"There has been a bit of an incident in the library."

"Incident? What kind of incident?"

The man smiled. I continued looking him over for any clue about who he was. There was a familiarity with his eyes, soft brown like that of a sparrow's feather, but I still couldn't place where I'd seen him before. "The Drakes will fill you in. Is there anything you need while you wait? A blood bag, perhaps?" He smiled softly.

"No, I'm fine. Thank you."

The man nodded but didn't leave the room.

"What is it?" I asked.

"The room. How do you like the changes?" I glanced around, but didn't notice much other than a different comforter on the bed. "It's nice," I responded, unsure of the reaction he was looking for.

"And the painting?"

I turned to look at the painting and stepped toward it. This image was seared into my memory, as it was one of the first things I had seen after transforming. When I had risen from the bed, I had lost control of my senses and had focused on this painting. It had been a dizzying array of dots that eventually melded into a complete painting as I had regained my composure.

I raised a hand to the canvas and ran my fingertips over the textured surface. I followed the cerulean wave as it soared up into the night sky, the foamy whitecap the only contrast. "It is beautiful," I muttered. But when I turned my head, I realized I was talking to myself. The butler was gone, the door to the room closed.

I returned my attention to the artwork and recalled thinking I'd seen something hidden behind the brushstrokes, something resembling letters. I concentrated at the center of the painting but noticed nothing. I tilted my head in the other direction, but that didn't help. I pursed my lips, realizing I needed to adjust my senses as if easing into hunting mode. Doing so would allow my vampire vision to see things it couldn't when I was in full control of my senses. But that also meant that my hearing and sense of smell would be heightened, and if I happened to notice a human, well, who knew how I'd react. Hopefully Max's training would keep me on the straight and narrow. On the other hand, maybe I was overreacting. Given that the castle was located in the middle of nowhere, I rationalized I wouldn't risk my sobriety by being a little lax with my self-control. I could let my guard down a bit without consequence, as I doubted there were any mortals within a twenty-mile radius.

I rolled my head from side to side and cracked my back. Shaking out my arms at my sides, I took a deep breath and then stood still. I closed my eyes and let my hearing expand. I heard squirrels scampering in the woods and birds cawing high above. With another breath, I heard the wind weaving through trees and fluttering leaves. I opened my eyes and a million specks of blue, white, gray and black sparkled—the individual specks of color that together made up the larger painting.

"Whoa," I whispered.

The colored speckles swirled in place while errant flecks zoomed off in opposite directions, bouncing around like Ping-Pong balls. When a speck reached the perimeter of the canvas, it boomeranged back and released more particles upon impacting the mass of color in the canvas's center.

I extended my left hand, and the specks responded by gathering to the spot where my hand was extended. I hesitated and then placed my hand on the canvas.

My touch scattered the particles, but they immediately rebounded and collected around my hand, pulsing in rhythm with my heartbeat. I drew my fingertips in toward my palm until all five tips touched. The pool of color followed my movement. I extended my fingers, and the colors reacted in kind. Pulling my fingertips together once again, I pulled my hand away from the canvas and to my surprise the specks followed, appearing as if they were connected by invisible glue adhered to my fingertips. I pulled my hand back farther, and the colors stretched with me, thinning the farther I moved from the canvas. I pulled my hand back to my head to see how far the colors would extend. The mass initially followed but then snapped back and splattered onto the canvas. Individual specks raced over the canvas, bouncing off of each other and the edges. Their speed increased, and the colors blurred into streaks before the gray, blue and white specks retreated to the edge, leaving a black swirling mass in the middle. The black paint ebbed and flowed like an oil slick bobbing on a wave before breaking off into six smaller groupings. Starting from the left, the paint began to spell words, the next group forming a word after the one to its left was completed.

Cursive writing scrawled letters as if written by an invisible force with pen in hand. I watched as the message revealed itself: *The truth will set you free*. I murmured the phrase out loud and wondered what it could mean.

The door opened and broke my concentration. "Allison, what are you doing in here?" Max asked.

I yelped and reigned in my senses. "Good Lord, Max, you scared the daylights out of me." I placed a hand over my heart and walked over to Max and hugged him. "The butler told me to wait for you here."

"The butler? Who? We sent all of the staff home hours ago when we first found out about…." Max dropped his head and pinched the bridge of his nose.

"I'm so sorry Max. What happened to Felix?"

"Not here. Let's go into the library where the others are waiting."

Max placed a hand on my lower back, steering me out of the room. I glanced over my shoulder at the painting. No swirling colors were there; no hidden message was exposed. It looked just as it had when I first entered the room–a painting of a storm over the ocean.

"You like the painting?" Max asked, stopping at the threshold.

"Um, yeah. It caught my attention the first time I was in this room. There's something about it that draws me to it.""It was one of Felix's favorites."

"Felix's favorites? Really?"

"Yes. It was given to him centuries ago. Felix always said it was special."

"Special? How so?"

"It's a trinket of sorts, akin to what you might know as the Magic 8 Ball."

I laughed. "You mean the plastic version of a billiard ball that you ask a question, flip over and find a message?"

"Yes, sort of. The painting was cast with magic and reveals sayings or pictures to anyone who has the ability to read it. Whereas the modern-day toy only has 20 responses, and the one you get is up to the luck of the draw, the painting can supposedly sense who is viewing it and deliver a personalized message. Felix was convinced it revealed some sort of foretelling. Did you see anything?"

I looked at the painting again and then back at Max. *The truth will set you free* echoed in my head. I didn't know the meaning behind the message and didn't want to detract from the situation that had brought me to the castle so I lied. "No, I didn't see anything."

Max sighed. "Not everyone can. Felix was the only one of us who could."

"Hmm," I mused as we exited the room. "Who gave him the painting?"

"A friend." Max picked up his pace and led me down the hallway.

"A friend with magical abilities?"

"Felix never said much about the gifter or the origin of the painting."

"And you never asked?"

"No."

"And you don't find it the least bit suspicious that Felix had a friend who gave him a magical painting?"

We stopped in front of two wooden doors that extended to the ceiling and were the width of the wall. Forged metal handles were the only decoration.

"Sometimes Allison, some things are better left unsaid, especially in the world of vampires."

I nodded, indicating I understood. The less Felix's siblings knew about the origin of the painting and who gifted it, the better for everyone involved. Max grabbed one handle and leaned into the door to open it. I followed behind.

"What happened in here?" I asked, surveying the room.

Bookshelves lay toppled on the floor and leather-bound books were strewn everywhere. Torn tapestries dangled over the stained-glass windows. I picked up a book and examined it. The volume was bound in dark green leather, its metal clasp broken. Fanning through pages of beautiful handwriting—flowing lines and swooping letters reminiscent of another day and age—and realized what I was looking at. I lifted my head and looked at Max.

"These are Vincent's, aren't they? They look exactly like the books he placed at my home in Ridge Hollow. The binding, the clasp, the writing—they're his, right?"

"Yes, Allison. This is our library and these," Max picked up a book and held it, "are Vincent's historical accounts. Anything and everything he witnessed first-hand or through the minds of others are documented here. Well, here and of course in the books at your house, as you mentioned." Max took the book from my hand and dropped it along with the book he had grabbed. "Come on," he said, waving me to follow him.

We walked farther into the cavernous room, navigating around tossed tables and chairs and more overturned bookshelves and books. We arrived at the far wall where a fire crackled in the hearth. Vincent, Marlo and Lorenzo sat at a wooden table, thumbing through books.

"What happened?" I asked again.

"That's what we'd all like to know," Vincent responded. He stood, grabbed my hand and kissed it.

I instinctively pulled my hand back and quickly looked around to see if anyone noticed my reaction. Marlo didn't acknowledge it verbally, but her squinty eyes indicated she was more observant than I preferred at the moment.

"Someone broke into the castle," Marlo responded.

"How is that possible?" I challenged. "You have a state-of-the-art security system."

"Yes, a security system built by Felix," Lorenzo chimed in. "One we're still trying to figure out. Whoever did this knew what they were doing and how to get around the system."

"What did they take?"

"We're not sure," Marlo said. "Look at this mess. It'll take us months to sort through these books and get them back in chronological order. We don't know if they took a book, multiple books, pages from a book… we don't know anything." Venomous tears spilled from her violet eyes.

I rushed to her side. "Hey, don't cry. We'll figure this out together." I dabbed her tears with a tissue I'd pulled from my pocket, the material singeing upon contact with the venom.

"We know one thing," Lorenzo said.

"What's that?" I asked as I threw the charred tissue into the fireplace. "Whatever they wanted was in this room. Nothing was disturbed elsewhere in the castle."

"And we know something else," Vincent added.

"What would that be?" I asked, trying to suppress the ill will I felt for him. As much as I didn't want to be around Vincent, I had to be the bigger person given the situation.

"Whoever did this didn't leave a trace. They left nothing behind, not even a scent a vampire could detect."

"So what are you saying? A vampire did this?"

"Possibly. Or someone who knew how to circumvent vampire senses."

"Who then, if not vampires? What other theories do you have?" "Angels, maybe. Or gypsies."

"We don't know who or what did this," Lorenzo interjected,

slamming a fist to the table. "All we know is that it wasn't a human. There's no way a mortal could bypass our security, ransack this library and not leave behind something we could use to identify him."

"Or her," Vincent added.

Lorenzo sighed and shook his head. Apparently I wasn't the only one not in the mood for Vincent's antics.

"The butler didn't hear anything?" I asked.

"The butler? No, they were all sent home hours ago," Marlo said through sniffles. She continued before I could mention anything about the butler who had escorted me upstairs. "It wouldn't have mattered even if they were here. I didn't hear anything, and I was here when it happened. How could I have not heard anything? I'm a vampire, and this happened in my home while I was here."

"Sister," Max said as he rubbed Marlo's shoulders. "Stop beating yourself up over this. You had no reason to suspect someone in the house, so your senses wouldn't have been heightened."

"Is this related to what happened to Felix?" I asked.

Marlo crumpled her face trying to hold back another round of tears from temporarily scarring her flesh. Max scratched her back in an attempt to soothe her.

"The timing is uncanny," Vincent responded. "It has to be related."

"On that, we agree. Please, sit." Lorenzo extended his hand to a vacant chair that Max had pulled out for me. Max sat in the other empty chair.

"What happened to Felix?" I asked, scanning the somber faces of those sitting around the table.

"We don't know," Lorenzo said.

"What do you mean? You don't know who killed him?"

"We definitely don't know that, Allison," Max responded. "But it's the way in which he was killed that has us stumped."

"There's only one way to kill a vampire," I challenged. "You rip out his throat and stake him through the stomach. That's what you taught me.""And that is true," Lorenzo said. "But apparently someone has discovered another way to kill our species."

"What do you mean?"

"Felix was shot, killed with wooden bullets," Marlo blurted out.

"Wooden bullets? But how?"

"We don't know," Max said and dropped his head in defeat.

"Wooden bullets are the sort of thing you see in today's TV shows or in folklore or in mortal's imaginations."

"We know," Lorenzo said, sighing as if they'd all already had this conversation.

"How can a measly piece of wood kill an immortal?"

"That's the question we all have, Allison," Vincent responded.

"We're guessing the bullet is spelled," Marlo said.

"Spelled? As in a gypsy spell?"

"Possibly."

"Possibly?" I challenged. "Who else do we know can cast spells? After seeing what gypsies are capable of, you know, with the whole casting a spell to unlock a portal to the Garden of Eden, should there be any doubt the gypsies are behind this?"

"We cannot afford to rush to judgment," Lorenzo cautioned. "If we were to retaliate now, it would set off an epic battle between us and the gypsies. We've done that once before, and it didn't end well for either side."

"You're referring to the vampire attack on their tribe in the early days, before you knew what the gypsies were capable of?" I recalled the story the Drakes had shared with me earlier this year. Prior to the creation of their sect of vampire society, vampires freely attacked humans. They made the mistake of attacking a band of gypsies who in turn used their influence over nature's elements to kill many of the vampires that had attacked them. A truce was eventually achieved whereby vampires promised to not attack gypsies in return for the gypsies' silence about the existence of vampires. It was a truce that had kept the peace for thousands of years, until, possibly, now.

"Yes." Lorenzo rested his chin in the palms of both hands and massaged his temples.

"But–"

"There are no 'buts,' Allison," Lorenzo mumbled. "We need to ascertain who did this before we take any action. Before starting a battle of that magnitude, we need to ensure we have found the true culprit."

We sat in silence. Max fixated on the fire. Marlo flipped through a book. Vincent stood and righted a toppled bookshelf, causing a bit of a raucous as he kicked books out of his way.

"Can I see him?" I murmured.

Lorenzo raised his head and looked at me.

"Can I see Felix?" I asked again.

"There will be a funeral in a couple of days. You can pay your respects then," Lorenzo said.

I smiled. "I can appreciate that, but I'd like to have a moment alone with him now, if I may."

Lorenzo's eyes flitted around the table at his siblings. I couldn't read the expression on any of their faces but couldn't imagine what objection they might have. Unless of course they knew something they weren't letting onto. *The truth will set you free* scrolled through my mind again.

"Come on," I pleaded. "What's the harm?"

"Fine," Lorenzo said. He stood from his chair and stretched. "Max, take her to see Felix."

Chapter 4

"Who found him?" I asked Max as we exited the library and walked toward the staircase.

"Marlo."

"How? Where?"

Max sighed. "Felix had been missing in action for two days. We knew he'd gone hunting, but the trip shouldn't have taken him as long as it appeared to be taking. He wasn't responding to any of our calls or messages, which really concerned us." Max glanced back with the look of a father scolding a child.

"Sorry," I sheepishly replied, realizing my unresponsiveness earlier in the day had caused the Drakes unneeded concern. "Ignoring your calls this morning probably didn't help things."

"Definitely not. We weren't sure if Felix's murder was an isolated incident or if someone was targeting us. But we found you via your cellphone signal, the same way Marlo located Felix. We saw that you were at your house in Ridge Hollow and then at your former home in Buzzard Hill." Max raised his eyebrows and peered down at me. There was that fatherly look again.

"Ah, yeah, I was."

"Mmm hmm. You know you're going to piss off the angels if you don't leave Matt alone."

"Where did Marlo find Felix, Max?" I asked, purposely changing the topic.

"In the Metroparks."

"The Metroparks? Where?"

"Near Buzzard's Roost, to be exact."

We arrived in the great room and rounded the corner, our footsteps echoing off the stone walls.

"What was Felix doing at the Buzzard's Roost? Was that where his hunt was supposed to have happened?"

"No, Allison. We wouldn't hunt for humans that close to home or in such a public area. There are too many joggers and cars passing through for that sort of thing, and you know we never feed on prey in our backyard. We don't know what Felix was doing there. Marlo found his body inside the perimeter of the tree line at the far end of the field."

"So not even close to the parking lot or the walking trails."

"Nope."

We walked through the dining room and kitchen into a hallway leading to the staff quarters. I didn't realize where we were headed, as all I could think about was what Felix could have possibly been doing at Buzzard's Roost.

The area was part of the Metroparks system, but aside from the annual Buzzard's Day festivities, not much went on at that particular location. It was a field the size of three football fields filled with tall grasses and brush. The land sloped into a valley with a creek before rising back up on the other side. The brush and rocky terrain made it difficult to navigate, and in fact, park goers were prohibited from entering the area. A variety of trees and shrubs bordered the field and extended for miles. It was all useless parkland except to the animals that lived there. The familiar sound of a specific doorknob rattling brought me back to reality. I grabbed Max's hand which was already turning the knob.

"Where are we going?" I asked, my voice trembling as a pit formed in my stomach. I already knew the answer but had to ask anyway.

"Allison, I'm sorry. Felix is in the cellar."

"You mean the dungeon?" I snapped.

"I know you don't have the fondest of memories from the time you spent down there –"

"From the time you held me captive down there," I corrected. Flashes of my captivity skipped through my mind–the hunger pains, the agony of being weaned off of human blood, my relentless calls for relief that went unanswered for days.

Max had no response as he looked at me with regret-filled eyes. I inhaled, knowing full well none of this was his fault. Had I not run off in the first place, he could have taught me the proper hunting protocol so I wouldn't have become a blood junkie–a crazed vampire who only found satisfaction with each mortal kill and who was propelled to the next kill from the high she had received from the previous one.

"Max, I know you did what you had to do in order to break my addiction to human blood, but I don't need to go back down there and relive those horrid memories."

"If you want to see Felix in private before the funeral, this is the only way."

I sighed and ran a hand through my hair. The last time I was down there, I had been tricked, and that deceit resulted in 66 days of captivity–the amount of time it took Max to break me of my addiction.

Before Vincent and I ran off to Paris, Max had pleaded with both of us to stay so he could help me get my urges under control. Max presented a good case–not only was he the hunter in the family–the one who monitored mortal kills and plotted the next in an effort to conceal our existence–but he was also the most experienced in helping vampires who needed to get their act together and their appetite in check. Max insisted proving to the Ruling Council that I was serious about concealing vampire existence from the mortal world by adhering to the sect's strict hunting protocols was the only way to get the Council off my back. But, Vincent fluffed him off by promising to take care of me, and I, of course, acted like a love-sick teenager who couldn't think for herself and went along with whatever my creator wanted.

Vincent and I gallivanted around Paris, Monaco, the Canary Islands and Greece. Vincent was aware of my raging appetite for human blood, having pulled me out of sticky situations on multiple occasions, but he ignored the severity of the situation. He was diligent about following Max's regimented hunting schedules and ensuring I went along and fed. But those trips weren't enough to satisfy my thirst. So I snuck off for a snack here and there, but apparently I wasn't as stealthy as I'd thought. Max was keeping tabs on us (tabs on me was probably more like it), and he quickly caught on to my illicit activities. Max confronted Vincent about my behavior, and in true Vincent fashion, he was reluctant to believe Max at first. Of course he didn't believe Max; Vincent thought he alone could help me–save me. That was until both of them caught me red-handed with a young man in my fangs in an alley behind a seedy Grecian nightclub. At the time, I didn't know they were spying on me. Vincent said nothing when I returned to our hotel room. In fact, he distracted me in the way only he knew best–with his body and his many boudoir talents. When we woke the next morning, Vincent said we had to return to Castle Adena to start planning the Drake's annual Halloween party. I questioned the timing, as the middle of May seemed much too early to start thinking about Halloween. But Vincent sold me the story. It was a combination of the creator's bond plus what I had seen firsthand at last year's party–the extravagant decorations, the sheer number of guests—that made me believe his lie.

"Allison? Do you want to see Felix or not?"

"Um…" *The truth will set you free* popped into my mind. Could that message have something to do with Felix's murder? The timing, like the library vandalism, was uncanny. I rationalized it was more important to see Felix one last time before the formality of a funeral to see if I could discover any clues. It was the least I could do for a fallen brother. "Yes, I want to see Felix."

Max opened the door and flipped a switch, illuminating oil torches affixed to the wall. We descended the staircase into the damp bowels of the castle. As my foot landed on the first stone step, I recalled Max's request back in May—his decoy to get me into the cellar—to help him retrieve some of the planning documents from the prior year's party.

Max stopped at the bottom step. I hadn't noticed and ran into him.

"Allison, are you okay?"

"Terrific," I replied sarcastically.

Max eyed me from head to toe, the corners of his mouth curving down. I grimaced, attempting to appease him. It must have worked; he turned the corner, and I followed. One look down the never-ending hallway and I spotted *the* door—sixth door down on the right in a row of twenty rooms that served as holding cells. I squeezed my eyes shut hoping that by avoiding the sight, the memories wouldn't resurface. But that backfired.

I recalled walking down the corridor ahead of Max. From behind, he directed me to the room. I pulled the door open and entered. I walked a few steps and looked around, perplexed as to why I was standing in an empty room. Where were the boxes of documents we were to retrieve? Max kept calling out, telling me what to look for. As I turned to reenter the hallway and to shout that there was nothing in the room, two hulking vampires, the size of professional wrestlers, descended from the corners of the ceiling. Each grabbed an arm and wrestled me into submission, securing my wrists and ankles with metal shackles. Their mission complete, they exited the room, and Max slammed the metal door shut. The sound of the latch grating over metal and twisting into place was a sound I would never forget. That was day one of Max's version of vampire rehab.

I opened my eyes and found myself standing in front of that very room. Max walked ahead unaware I had stopped. I placed my hands on the door and peered through the narrow slit, the only way to see into or out of the space. Shackles hung lifeless against the wall. I stared at the torturous devices that had delivered volts of electricity to stun me into submission. At the time, it hadn't taken me long to figure out my movements caused the electrical charges. I had sat there in stunned silence, not believing what had just happened. Vincent had lured me back to the castle. Max had lured me into the cellar. I had been ambushed and incarcerated. After a few minutes, Max had reappeared, apologizing, saying this was the only way to cure me and keep the Ruling Council off of my back for Sam and Brian's unsolved murders–crimes I'd committed which were still front and center in the news. If the Council's suspicions that I'd revealed the existence of vampires to the mortal world were heightened, the Council would want my head. Therefore, Max said I needed to deprive myself of human blood in order to control my urge for it. Then Vincent had appeared, that damned coward. He apologized profusely for misleading me but said this was for the best, that it had to be done. I cursed him and told him I never wanted to see him again. His betrayal was unforgivable in my eyes. How could the one who claimed to have loved me so much deceive me like this and treat me this way?

I gulped at the recollection of what had happened in the days that followed. Unanswered hunger pains had pierced my stomach, each stab like a fresh knife wound, the venom in my system like salt being rubbed into that wound. My mouth was a desert filled with unbearable dryness, and my tongue thrashed like a flame begging for relief that never came. But that pain and discomfort paled in comparison to the mummification of my body. With each passing day, the life force drained from every cell in my body. I was later told that was the venom receding to my belly to hibernate and lay dormant, waiting for a splash of blood to waken it and bring it back to life. From cell to vein to muscle, every square inch of my body solidified until I resembled the monster in my nightmares. The first night I had spent with Vincent on Rattlesnake Island, before I knew I was the first of Cain's half-mortal/half-vampire offspring to exhibit signs of vampirism, I dreamt I was in a desolate forest. I had an undeniable hunger yet I wasn't able to stand, let alone search, for nourishment. I crawled to a puddle where I saw my reflection. What I saw was a mummified version of me. Fast forward to my time in this prison cell as I witnessed my arms, hands and legs turning into a hard bronzed exterior. But my mind? Well it was perfectly intact. Although I was immobile, I still had all of my faculties. I was attuned to what was happening as I became painfully entombed in my own body.

Several days passed before Felix entered the cell to feed me. I didn't know if he drew the short stick for this assignment or was assigned via process of elimination as Vincent and Max were two of the last people I wanted to see. The smell of blood snapped me back to consciousness, and honestly I would have been happy with whoever was bringing me nourishment. But it wasn't the type of blood I craved. It was animal blood. I gagged, as it wasn't the elixir my taste buds desired, but when one was starved–famished –one wasn't picky.

Felix coaxed me through it, stroking my hair, telling me all would be okay, that my body needed the nourishment in order to return back to normal. Unable to swallow, the liquid slid down my throat, awakening the evil that resided in my stomach. Blood nourished the venom that slowly began traveling throughout my body, waking dormant cells. My limbs tingled, regaining life and their normal appearance. As I finished one blood bag, Felix tore open another and pressed it to my lips, telling me I was doing a good job but that I needed more blood. My strength returning, I clutched the bag and pressed it to my mouth, sucking harder, unable to get the liquid in my system fast enough, relishing the way my body felt as it regained normalcy. The venom moved faster, depositing relief at all of my nerve endings until I was once again a fully functioning vampire–a fully functioning vampire who wasn't overcome with the need for human blood.

"Allison," Max called out.

"Huh," I muttered as I woke from my daydream.

"This way." He offered a small wave and turned down a corridor.

I caught up to him and he turned. Grabbing my arm, he asked, "Are you sure you're okay?"

I bit my lip and nodded.

"Listen, Allison, I am sorry."

"Max, stop. It was my fault I ran off and naively thought I could handle vampire life on my own or believed Vincent could have helped me. I'm the one who binged on human blood. You and Felix and Marlo and Lorenzo, well you all did what you had to do to save me from myself and the wrath of the Ruling Council. You had to do what you did to get my urges in check."

"Vincent too. You need to give him a break, Allison. He loves you, and although he may not have been thinking logically at first, he came around to his senses and did what he had to do to help you."

"Max, don't stick your nose where it doesn't belong." I didn't need dating advice from Max; although I could somewhat understand how he'd defend his brother.

Max smiled. "But –"

"But," I cut him off, "detox was hands down the worst experience of my life following my transformation. I've never experienced agony like that. It's not something I'm going to forget easily. It's surreal being back down here after all that happened a few short months ago."

"Yes, and now you're down here for another unpleasant reason."

"Yeah, Felix. Where is he?"

"Come." Max waved, and I followed.

The door scraped against the concrete floor as Max pushed it open. The room was pitch black, but my vampire vision allowed me to see Felix lying on a metal table, the kind you'd expect to see in a coroner's office, in the center of the room.

I walked to the table and set my hand on the metal. Words escaped me. Felix looked just like Felix. His usually pallid complexion was unchanged, giving the appearance he was resting and not a corpse. I ran a finger over his cheek and felt an unnatural warmness for a vampire. Our body temperatures fluctuated between numbingly cold and blazingly hot, never room temperature like he was now.

"He looks like he's resting," I whispered.

Florescent lights buzzed to life overhead, and Max walked up behind me.

"I know. He looks like he's going to say something at any given moment, doesn't he?"

"Mmm hmm."

Felix was still clothed in what I assumed he had been wearing when he died. His boots and the bottom of his jeans were muddied, his jacket flapped open at his sides. A Rolex ticked away, keeping time Felix no longer needed to worry about.

"Why are his boots muddy?"

"We're guessing Felix may have tried to flee his attacker, possibly running through the valley and the creek to get to the other side of Buzzard's Roost where Marlo found his body."

I grabbed Felix's jacket and pulled it away from his body. "Where are the bullet wounds?"

"He was shot in the back," Max said.

I snorted. "Damn cowards."

"Step aside. I'll show you."

I backed away from the table as Max laid Felix's left arm over his chest and slid his hands under Felix's side to roll him on his right side. "Look, but don't touch."

I inched closer, bending to see the mortal wounds. I lifted Felix's jacket to get a better look and spotted three holes in his white shirt, the tattered border blackened as if burnt. I lifted the shirt and gasped when I saw the bullets lodged in his back. Three round wooden bullets were flush with Felix's skin as if stopped upon entry.

"Max, we can't leave the bullets in him." I brushed my thumb over one of the wooden bullets and yelped in pain.

"You touched it?" Max yelled as he rolled Felix onto his back. "I told you not to."

"Damn, that burns." I rubbed my thumb with my right hand. The reddened skin looked like it had been scalded, the wood grain etched into my print.

"No kidding." Max raised his hand. "I learned the hard way as I tried to extract the bullets."

I grabbed Max by the wrist and inspected the wounds imprinted into his flesh. "What about a tool?" I dropped his arm. "We have to have something around here that we can use to remove the bullets." I glanced around the room but there was nothing else in it.

"We tried, Allison, but nothing worked. I got frustrated and tried to pull them out with my bare hands and that's how I got these." Max wiggled his fingers. Scars were on both thumbs, index and middle fingers.

"Jesus, Max. Who did this?"

"Don't know, but we'll figure it out. That's part of why we asked you to come back here today, to help with the investigation. Well that and we were also concerned when we discovered you were at Matt's."

"What does that have to do with any of this?" My blood pressure skyrocketed. It was none of the Drakes' business if I had been at Matt's house.

"Angels and vampires are enemies as you well know, and as you heard earlier, we weren't sure if Felix's murder was an isolated incident or if we were under attack. We don't know who we can trust, all of our enemies included. And since you're not supposed to be cavorting with Matt, we weren't sure if you were there of your own free will or not."

"I was there of my own free will," I defended.

"That'll be a topic of conversation for another time.""What next?" I asked hurriedly, trying to change the subject."First, we bury our brother. Then we figure out who did this and make them pay."

Chapter 5

The TV served as background noise distracting my mind from the day's upcoming event. It was better than the alternative–sitting in a quiet house where my mind would focus on the morbid event about to unfold. I sat on the edge of the couch playing with the hem of my dress, twisting and untwisting the black fabric around my finger. I dreaded Felix's funeral. Who enjoyed going to such an affair? But it was necessary. It was a final goodbye to a brother and dear friend.

The past two days had been filled with funeral preparations. I'd learned that while such events weren't customary for vampires, they also weren't uncommon. If the deceased left specific instructions about funeral arrangements, then relatives would carry those out. Felix had previously expressed his desire for a small gathering followed by interment at Riverside Cemetery. I thought it a very human-like request, and that gave me comfort. Though we vampires were monsters, maybe there was a part of that human being we once were that we never lost. Although small, it was much needed comfort, a stark contrast to the message written on the slip of paper tucked into the envelope that I'd placed on the end table.

I couldn't move my eyes away from the manila stationary that contained a final message from Felix. It had been delivered via courier last night and had kept me awake all night as I had tried to decipher its meaning. The straightforward message was chilling; it had stopped me in my tracks as I read it. I wasn't sure how I was going to act normal around the Drakes after having read Felix's warning.

The sound byte announcing a news update filtered through the speakers and broke my concentration. I fiddled with my dress but tuned a curious ear to hear if the anchor had anything newsworthy to share.

"Good Morning, Steve," the female reporter greeted. "Local police say there are no new leads in the murder of Sam Thornberg, the man whose body was discovered here this past March."

A jolt ran through my body when I heard Sam's name. I stopped playing with my dress, stood and walked closer to the TV. The blonde reporter stood in front of a sign for Edgewater Park, a local beach west of downtown Cleveland.

"Sam," I whispered. A professional photo, maybe a high school senior year picture, flashed on the screen. Sam's sandy brown hair swept to one side, and a dimple punctuated the opposite cheek. The screen flipped to a picture of Sam in a tux and bowtie with an attractive blonde in a green formal gown. The screen returned to the reporter.

"If you recall, a massive manhunt took place after Sam failed to show up for work on March 15. Sam's truck was later discovered in Buzzard Hill, over thirty miles away from this area, but Sam's body was discovered in a sewer drain located near here. The drain funnels water from the Rocky River into Lake Erie. Sam was the son of Councilman Thornberg who has served the city of Rocky River for over twelve years. Sam's family says they'll continue to pressure police until Sam's killer is found."

The screen panned left to a man dressed in a gray suit. His matching gray hair was combed over in a futile attempt to conceal his baldness. The reporter stuck the microphone in front of his double-chinned face.

"We will not rest until Sam's killer is brought to justice,"

Councilman Thornberg bellowed into the mic. A small gathering of people shouted 'no' as they emphatically shook their heads. "As any family would in this situation, we want answers. Why Sam? What did he do to deserve this?"

"He was in the wrong place at the wrong time," I responded. I scanned the crowd that had gathered behind Councilman Thornberg. My eyes settled on a young woman who resembled the female in what I presumed was Sam's prom picture. Her eyes held back tears. Her lower lip quivered. Her cheeks were sallow, and she leaned on another woman for support. I wondered if she was Sam's girlfriend. A pang of guilt pierced my mind. I'd taken away her friend, her lover. I looked at some of the other people around her; all of the other people who I'd robbed of a friend, a son, a companion. I hadn't just taken Sam away from them; I had damned Sam's soul for all of eternity. I wrapped an arm around my midsection as if that would comfort me.

"But most of all," Sam's father continued, "we want his killer brought to justice."

"And that would be me," I muttered and turned away from the TV.

Sam had been driving to work the morning I escaped captivity on Rattlesnake Island. Once on the mainland, I needed a ride so I hitchhiked, persuading Sam to let me in his truck. Once inside, I couldn't resist the smell of his blood. His musky scent awakened the evilness within my core, and I couldn't suppress my appetite. I closed my eyes and rubbed my temples as I recalled how out of control I was back then. Why couldn't I have seen then how out of hand I was? I needed to feed, and Sam, unfortunately for him, became my meal.

I had left Sam for dead in the hotel room I'd convinced him to rent. The horny little bastard thought he was going to get lucky but had no idea what was about to happen to him. I hadn't thought of him much more thereafter until my final meeting with the Ruling Council. Once

Vincent had been cleared of the charges of transforming me into a vampire without my permission, the Council's attention turned to the rumors they'd heard about my cross-country killing spree. I pleaded my case that I was cautious of whom I had killed and when and where so as not to draw attention to the existence of vampires, and Felix had backed me up with newspaper clippings and footage of those kills. No unwarranted attention had been garnered. The crimes had been labeled as random acts or unsolved mysteries. Then I remembered Sam, and Brian, the cook at Scavenger's Bar & Grille who I had killed later that same day. I had been careless with those kills, so wrapped up in trying to get Matt to talk to me and explain why we couldn't be together that I didn't cover my tracks. I had promised the Council I'd get my appetite under control and promised myself I'd go back to the scenes of those two crimes to conceal what I'd done. My promise was enough to appease the Council at the time, but I was sure their patience was wearing thin with the non-stop news coverage that was as prevalent today as it had been six months ago.

The reporter jumped back in. "It's absolutely puzzling how few clues there are in this crime. No witnesses have come forward in either case, and there are no new leads. And there's still the mystery about how Sam's truck got all the way to Buzzard Hill and who drove the vehicle there. Police and FBI combed over the vehicle, but no evidence was found. The odd connection, of course, is that Brian Foster was also killed on March 15. Coincidence? The police don't think so. Sergeant Daley, tell us why you think the same person may have killed both Sam and Brian."

The camera panned right to a uniformed police officer. He was about the same height as the reporter and appeared to be in his early thirties, his graying hair buzzed short beneath his peaked cap. "Well Monica, as you know from previous reports, Sam and Brian did not know each other, and their deaths, other than occurring on the same day, have nothing in common. Sam was found in a drain pipe, the cause of death a broken neck, and Brian's body was found, neck slit, in a landfill after presumably having been tossed in the dumpster behind Scavenger's, the local Buzzard Hill bar where Brian worked as a cook. But the link between the two is Sam's truck appearing in Buzzard Hill the same day Sam went missing and Brian was killed. That's too much of a coincidence to overlook. With all of the people in attendance at the Buzzard's Day festivities in Buzzard Hill, we feel strongly someone had to have seen something out of place. Maybe someone saw who was driving Sam's truck. Maybe someone saw Brian on his smoke break. Whatever you may have seen, please, we urge you no matter how small or inconsequential you think it might be, call the police. Call the police and let us do our job."

The camera panned back to Monica. "Six months later, both towns, Rocky River and Buzzard Hill, are still on edge after these murders. Any information leading to the arrest of the monster who committed these crimes would be appreciated. One thing is for sure: with the political clout of Councilman Thornberg and the small community of Buzzard Hill demanding justice for their beloved cook, police will not stop until the killer is found."

Grabbing the remote control, I turned off the TV. The media attention certainly wasn't helping my case in the eyes of the Ruling Council. As long as the media threat persisted, the more the Council's paranoia would grow that I'd revealed our existence to the outside world. Not only that, but members of their covens knew what was transpiring, and if I was allowed to get away with my crimes, why couldn't they? The Council couldn't afford legions of vampires acting out of turn and further exposing our existence. Though the Council had been apprised of my detox and subsequent sobriety, I doubted those actions would go far as long as Sam and Brian's murder cases were still alive and well in the press.

The doorbell chimed. I grabbed my wrap and purse and headed for the door. Marlo had said a driver would be here to pick me up at 10:30, and the driver was right on time. I pulled open the door and froze at the sight of my visitor.

"Matt? What are you doing here?"

"Hey, Ali," he smirked, shifting his weight. "You, uh, rushed off the other day without these." He held up two square canvases covered with dried rose petals—the artwork that served as my excuse to visit him the other day.

"Oh," I said. I had completely forgotten about my request given what had happened to Felix. "Come in."

Matt walked into the foyer and surveyed the area as I surveyed him. He looked mighty fine in his khaki cargo shorts and green plaid button down, the collar flopped down and in serious need of ironing. This was his first time here. I had told him about this place when we had met back in July. I had invited him to swing by and check it out sometime as I thought he'd love the area since it was the type of town he had always wanted to move to. That visit never happened thanks to a meddling Gabriela.

"Nice place." He walked into the living room.

"Thanks." I closed the door.

"It's kind of ironic."

"What's that?" I asked as I turned around.

"You living way out here and me living in the house you wanted. We're living where the other person had always wanted."

"Ahh, if you recall, Buzzard Hill wasn't exactly where I had wanted to live. I was hoping for a trendy downtown condo, remember? Buzzard Hill was a compromise."

"Huh, you're right. Since it wasn't the countryside retreat I had hoped for, I always considered it what you wanted."

I chuckled. "Funny how things sometimes work out, huh?"

"Can I set these here?" Matt pointed to the sofa table, empty except for the framed dried rose and a lamp.

"Yeah, that's fine. I'd forgotten there were two canvases. Thanks for bringing them over. I appreciate it, especially since I know Gabriela wouldn't take too kindly to you being here right now.""Gabriela doesn't control me," Matt snapped.

His sudden change in demeanor caught me off guard.

"Well then, I'm sure your girlfriend wouldn't be too happy knowing where you are either," I said, alluding to the brunette who had left his house when I had arrived the other day.

"I'm going to go." Matt moved toward the door.

"No, wait." I placed a hand on him and relished the feeling of his muscular chest beneath his shirt. I glanced up at his face and a wave of emotion swept through me as visions of our happier times flipped through my mind like a movie reel. "I'm sorry. I didn't mean to start anything. Stay for a moment?" A tear rolled from the corner of my eye.

"Hey, what's wrong?" Matt wiped the tear and I instinctively grabbed his hand to look for the venomous burn. He smiled at my reaction. "You forgot. Angels don't scar from vampire venom."

"Yeah, I guess I forgot." Tears sprung from my eyes like water out of a broken faucet. I turned away from Matt, wiping the tears with the back of my hands, dabbing at my eyes and trying not to smudge my eye makeup.

"Ali, what's going on?"

I wanted to unload my emotional baggage and tell him everything – Felix's murder, my probable demise if Sam and Brian's murders remained unsolved, and mostly my feelings for him. I couldn't mention anything about Sam or Brian. I was sure the truth would only confirm what Gabriela had likely told him about me; the truth would only disgust Matt and bring to life for him the monster I really was. And I definitely couldn't confess my feelings. He had been more than clear back in March that we were no longer married, and he had obviously moved on with the mysterious brunette. He apparently had had more time to grieve the passing of our relationship to get to the point where he could move on. I, on the other hand, had dealt with a stint in rehab that had derailed my life for two months. I hadn't had a chance to grieve the ending of our relationship although I'd been doing a pretty good job of trying to move past it by masquerading with Vincent. So I revealed the only thing I felt I could.

"It's Felix. He's dead."

"What?" Matt grabbed me from behind and twirled me around. "Vincent's brother?"

"You could say he was my brother too."

"I'm so sorry, Ali." He pulled me to him and hugged me. "What happened?"

I buried my head in Matt's chest and inhaled his scent. God, how I missed him. I had a brief flashback from when we were married of snuggling with his pillow when he wasn't home and breathing in his scent trapped in the fabric. How his cologne had filled my nostrils and how that scent somehow was adequate replacement for him when he couldn't physically be there. How holding a pillow that smelled like him somehow temporarily replaced him. And how in the past months, I couldn't fill that void no matter how hard I'd tried, or with whom I'd tried. Matt shifted away from me.

"He was shot. I got a call from Max when I was at your house the other day telling me Felix was dead. That's why I left without the artwork."

"Shot?"

"Yes."

"But how? A bullet is useless against a vampire."

"Not these bullets." I raised my hand to show him my scarred thumb.

Matt grabbed my wrist and inspected my thumb more closely. "What's this?"

"A burn. From one of the three bullets in Felix's back." "I don't understand." "Neither do we. Felix was shot with wooden bullets. The Drakes tried to extract them, but they're not removable. It frustrated Max so much that he tried removing them with his own hands and got burned. He warned me not to touch them, but I didn't listen."

Matt chuckled. "Bullheaded as always, huh?"

"I suppose," I said with a soft chuckle. "The scars appear permanent, odd considering vampires heal from all wounds."

Matt's eyebrows furrowed, a look of concentration on his face.

"What is it, Matt?"

"Huh? What? Um, nothing. I'm thinking. This is so strange."

"Who do you think could have done this?"

"How would I know?"

"Do you think an angel could have done this?" I pressed.

"Now why would you ask me something like that, Ali?"

"I don't know. You're deep in thought over there like you know something more than you're letting on."

"I certainly don't know who would have killed Felix. But I know it wouldn't have been an angel. We wouldn't instigate a war for no reason."

"But what if an angel caught Felix in the act of killing a mortal? Wouldn't an angel have killed him to save the mortal's soul?"

"When was Felix killed?"

"Three days ago."

"My flock hasn't been out on a mission to protect mortals from vampires in a few weeks."

"Your flock?""Yes. I have my own platoon of angels–we're called a flock–and I run my own missions."

"You're moving up the angel Army ranks, aren't you?"

"I guess you could say that. My rank also means I'm privy to information about other flocks. If Felix had been caught and punished by an angel, I certainly would have heard about it, especially given his relationship to a seated Ruling Council member."

"I don't know, Matt." I shook my head. "Something's not right."

"What do you mean?"

I walked to the end table, picked up the envelope and held it between two fingers. "I received this yesterday. A courier brought it last night."

"What is it?" Matt asked as he grabbed it.

"A letter. From Felix.""A letter from Felix?"

"Yep. Go ahead and read it."

Matt pulled the single sheet of paper out of the envelope and scanned it while murmuring the message.

"My Dearest Allison. If you've received this letter, something horrible has come of me. More than likely, I am dead. As you well know, I've been researching you ever since the onset of your vampirism. My curiosity has gotten the best of me, and I simply needed to know why you were the first of Cain's half mortal/half vampire descendants to exhibit signs of vampirism. I suspect the answer will also account for your superior strength for such a young vampire.

"As I've gotten closer to solving the mystery that is you, I've had a feeling I was being followed. Evilness lurked everywhere I went, and its

presence intensified the closer I got to solving this puzzle. I have answers, Allison, but am apprehensive to put pen to paper for fear the letter could be intercepted. Keep your eyes open, Allison. The truth will find you. And trust no one. Not even my siblings. Until we meet again, Felix."

Matt looked up from the note.

"I know, right? What the heck?"

"Is he saying one of his siblings killed him?""I don't know. I don't want to read too much into it. All he warns is to not trust them. But what do you think about the other part of the letter?"

Matt looked back down at the note in his hand. "He'd been researching you?"

"Yeah, but I already knew that. Ever since I first met the Drakes, I was a mystery to all of them, but Felix took the most interest. They all questioned how or why I was the first descendant to exhibit signs of vampirism, but Felix took it on as his personal mission to find out. Heck, I didn't even care that much. Sure it would be interesting to know, but did it matter in the end? Would it have changed how things ended up? He was the one focused on the Bible Code, thinking it would lead to answers. And it did… just not the answers he was looking for."

"Maybe that knowledge is worth something to someone. Maybe Felix uncovering that information was his death sentence."

"It would appear so."

"So now what?"

"Well, according to the Drakes, first we bury Felix, and then we find out who did this and make them pay."

"What if it was an angel? What kind of revenge would you exact?"

"Really, Matt? Are you worried we'd start a war by killing an angel in retribution?"

"Yeah. The thought crossed my mind."

"Felix is family. We will figure out who did this, and we will exact the appropriate punishment. You can't tell me that if an angel turned up dead with vampire bites on his neck that the angels wouldn't be out for justice.""Do you believe angels were behind this? Do you really believe that?"

"I don't know what to believe, Matt. Maybe it was the angels. Maybe it was the gypsies. All I know is I have to work with the Drakes to solve Felix's murder, not trusting any of them too much, while searching for whatever Felix uncovered about me."

"Sounds like you have a lot on your plate."

"Yes, I do. And I could use some help." I offered a soft smile.

"Ali, I can't."

"Why not?"

"Because –"

"You said Gabriela doesn't control you."

Matt's face flushed. "She doesn't control me."

"Good. So then nothing's stopping you from helping me."

The muscles in Matt's cheeks flexed as he clenched his jaw. He looked down at the floor and then up at me. "Allison, I can't help you. I wish I could, but I can't risk getting caught again. I've risked a lot just coming here today to give you the artwork."

I scanned his face, trying to understand what he was feeling. Was his loyalty to the Army that strong? Could I convince him to help me, his former wife, unearth clues that would finally answer why I was the first descendant to exhibit signs of vampirism and answer who had killed Felix?

"Fine. Whatever. I don't know when you turned into such a rule player. You're not the same person I once knew, Matthew Carmichael. Something in you has changed, and I don't know if it's for the better. The old Matt, the one I knew and loved, would have done anything to help a *friend* in need."

I opened the door and waited for him to leave. He stared at me with a blank expression before walking out. Stopping on the front porch, he turned. "Ali-gator, don't let us leave on this note."

"You're the one allowing us to leave on this note, not me."

I slammed the door shut.

Chapter 6

Tires hummed as the limo rolled over the asphalt road. That was the only sound. Other than initial pleasantries, neither the Drakes nor I had spoken during the trip to Riverside Cemetery. The gravity of Felix's funeral weighed heavily on me, and it was apparent by their silence and somber expressions that it weighed heavily on the Drakes as well. I hadn't asked, but wondered how many vampire funerals they had attended throughout the centuries. Although they'd said it wasn't an uncommon occurrence, I couldn't imagine them attending too many funerals, especially funerals for a sibling you'd had for over two millennia. It was hard to let go of a loved one—I knew since I'd done it seven years ago with both of my parents who passed away weeks apart from each other—and wondered if it was more difficult after knowing a person for thousands of years like the Drakes had known each other.

Though I'd only known Felix for about a year, I considered him family, and his death pained me. Aside from Marlo, he was the one Drake sibling I felt most comfortable around. Max always had me on edge. He seemed to be lurking around every corner ensuring I was still sober. Lorenzo was too serious. As the Drake family's seated member of the Ruling Council, he was always dealing with Council matters. Too much vampire politics was enough to sour the sweetest of demeanors. And then there was Vincent. Enough said.

Felix had had charm and charisma that could set anyone at ease, and he had been sincerely interested in each person he met. He had had a passion for wanting to understand the root cause of all things, me included. After realizing that, it came as no surprise Felix had been researching why I was the first descendant of an immortal Cain and his mortal lover to exhibit signs of vampirism. He had asked a lot of questions in his quest for answers, diving deeper than the information recorded in Vincent's accounts, but he never made me feel like a science experiment. His other passion was technology, and being the tech guru in the family, he had always ensured I had the latest gadgets to keep up with Max's hunting regimen and stay off of the angels' radar, and to track my diet in order to keep me on the straight and narrow. He was an old soul who was going to be missed.

As the limo rounded a corner, I turned my attention to the Drake siblings. Marlo's face was covered with a black veil in an attempt to conceal her tear-stained face. She wore a black dress with a short hem in front, long in the back and sat across from me. She stared blankly out the window. Lorenzo, his blond hair loose and flowing over his shoulders, sat stoically next to her with his hands folded in his lap and his eyes closed. Max sat next to Lorenzo and was occupied with his phone, mumbling something about hunting conditions in Canada. And Vincent sat next to me. Like a timid adolescent attempting to make a move, he had slowly inched his way closer until our legs touched. He gave an apprehensive smile, which I returned. I didn't recoil when he grabbed my hand. The solemnity of the day dictated that we needed to be here for each other to provide support. Looking at the melancholy demeanors, I couldn't understand why Felix had warned me to not trust any of them.

The limo passed through the Riverside Cemetery gates. The historic burial grounds were over 135 years old and served as the final resting place for famous Clevelanders, wealthy families and common folk alike.

It was also where my parents were interred.

The vehicle came to a stop, and we waited for the chauffer to open the door. As the door opened, Max tucked his phone inside his suit coat and darted for the door, stopping outside of the vehicle to offer Marlo a hand. Lorenzo followed.

"I know this is difficult for you," Vincent whispered in my ear before gently kissing my cheek.

"It's difficult for all of us."

Vincent smiled and rubbed my shoulder. "I wasn't talking about Felix's funeral. I know about the last time you were here."

I jerked my head. My jaw went slack. "But how did you...." And then realized I already knew the answer. "You were watching over me when my parents died?"

"I was."

"Were you at both funerals?"

"Yes, I watched from the chapel's choir loft."

I nodded my head in acknowledgement and wondered about all of the life events I'd experienced that Vincent and the Drakes had experienced with me but from afar. How much had they seen? I already knew Vincent had witnessed my birth. What else? My first day of school, my first boyfriend, my wedding? I suddenly felt like I had never had a shred of privacy my entire mortal life.

I removed my hand from Vincent's and slid over to the door where I grabbed Max's waiting hand. The moist, humid air was suffocating as I emerged from the vehicle, the air so thick it was like breathing heat. Once fully out of the limo, I stood and straightened my dress but hesitated to look at the chapel, the place where I had said my final goodbye to my parents. Instead I glanced down, looking right, then left. We were in the old part of the cemetery, the lawn dotted with enormous family plot markers, surrounded by smaller headstones for the deceased, unlike the newer area that only permitted flat headstones. There was something eerily romantic about the plot markers, each of them unique, the only commonality each family's surname carved into the stone in large letters. There were Celtic crosses, clusters of angels and mini gazebos all in different shades of gray cement, white stone and black marble. The occasional family mausoleum broke up the sculptures which otherwise stood like fine works of art in a museum. But there was nothing romantic about being here.

Vincent came up behind me and placed both of his hands on my shoulders. He pulled me to him and whispered, "I'm here for you."

I squeezed my eyes shut, thankful that, for this particular day at least, he was here. When I opened them, I gazed up at the Victorian chapel. Slivers of stained glass windows provided the only color on the charcoal stone exterior. A bell tower tolled a mournful hymn and punctuated black stained doors. Manicured flower beds filled with mums edged the building. I lifted my right hand to Vincent's left, tapped it and then walked toward the building.

The chapel was already filled with mourners. The space only accommodated 100, and it appeared as if all 100 vampires were already here. I looked around the room and recognized many of the faces from last year's Halloween party including the seated members of the Ruling Council. Titus was already looking at me when I spotted him. He squinted his transparent peridot-colored eyes and nodded his head in my direction, a gesture I returned. Lucretia stood next to him. I'd expected a cold reception from her given our history, if you could call it that. Vincent's jilted ex-lover, Lucretia had made her displeasure with having been dumped by him for a mortal known at the last Ruling Council meeting. The last thing I expected from her was a smile, but that's exactly what I got. Amil and Marguerite stood behind those two and whispered something amongst themselves while peering at me. As I tuned my hearing to eavesdrop, they clammed up. I heard nothing but had a pretty good idea what they were talking about given this morning's news coverage. The media needed to move on from Sam and Brian's unsolved murders; that was my only chance of getting out from under the Ruling Council's suffocating attention. I was sure my affiliation with Lorenzo was the only reason the Council hadn't already acted on a punishment they felt was far overdue.

The only mortals present were those employed by the cemetery, and they were none the wiser that they were surrounded by the Devil's greatest creation that could damn their souls for eternity in the blink of an eye. Right about now, I could hug Max for having tortured me in rehab. My stomach didn't so much as growl as I inhaled the humans' scent. The sight of their jugulars pulsing to the beat of their hearts underneath their skin didn't so much as entice me. I had restraint. I was in control, and I hoped that was evident to the four Ruling Council members watching my every move.

I squeezed through the crowd on my way to the front of the chapel where Felix lay in the coffin. The black coffin was lined with gray silk and crowned with a spray of purple miniature roses. I kneeled and instinctively made the sign of the cross – habit from my Catholic upbringing. I paused, unsure of what would happen to the Devil's spawn having made a symbolic gesture of his nemesis.

"Don't worry, you won't burst into flames," Vincent whispered as he knelt beside me.

I smiled, welcoming the humor for the fleeting levity it brought to the situation, my attention never leaving Felix. His pressed gray suit and black shirt were impeccable, not a wrinkle in sight. The amethyst tie provided a striking contrast against the suit and Felix's pallid complexion and brown hair. A gold tie clip with his initials glinted under the overhead light. I bowed my head and prayed that God forgive Felix for the sins he had committed as a vampire. Dying without your soul meant an eternity burning in Hell, at least until the End of Times, when as our coven believed we could beg God for forgiveness for what we'd done and hopefully be granted everlasting life. Felix didn't deserve an afterlife of pain and suffering. After all, he was one of God's creatures first before joining the Devil's brood. He was the lost sheep who was now returning home. I could only hope God would not forsake Felix and would absolve him of his sins, not permitting him to burn in the fiery depths of Hell.

"Felix really wanted this music?" I asked. I stood and glared at the organ that droned on with a somber hymn.

"He did," Vincent responded. "Are you okay?"

"Yeah, I'm fine."

"Are you?"

I cocked my head and had a feeling Vincent was talking about something other than the funeral. "Well, I'm still perplexed by who could have done this to Felix, but I suppose we'll find out soon enough."

"We will." There was a long pause and I used the break in conversation to scan the room. "Did you accomplish what you needed to the other day?"

"What?" I was keenly aware Vincent was alluding to me kicking him out of my house the same day I ended up on Matt's doorstep, the same day the Drakes discovered Felix had been murdered. I was sure that his siblings, desperate to find me after discovering Felix's body, had to have asked Vincent if he knew where I was given we'd been spending so much time together. I was also sure once they discovered that I wasn't at my home in Ridge Hollow, as Vincent would have confirmed since he had just left my house, they had told him my whereabouts. And knowing Vincent, he would have pressed his siblings for the exact location.

"You said you had something to take care of and it seemed pretty important to you. Important enough to throw me out and go at it alone."

I huffed and looked away. "I can't believe you want to talk about this, now." My eyes flitted over the room. I attempted to divert my anger by soaking in the somber expressions, as if absorbing the mourners' sadness would squelch my anger.

"Well there haven't been many opportunities between the funeral preparations and library clean up."

"And you couldn't wait a few more hours until the services were finished?"

One man caught my attention. He stood alone, leaning against the wooden frame of the side entrance. His brown hair fell to the middle of his back in soft waves, dirty blond highlights catching under the lighting. He was a vampire as evidenced by the gold flecks in his eyes. He held my gaze and remained motionless. Then in one fluid move, he turned and was out the door.

Vincent kept talking, unaware that I wasn't paying attention to him. I patted him on the chest and said, "I need some air."

"I'll come with you."

"No." I stopped and looked at him.

"But…"

"I need some water," I lied and fanned myself with a hand. "It's this heat."

Vincent eyed me suspiciously. I fluffed the top of my dress for dramatic effect, furthering the lie I needed to hydrate.

"Then allow me to get a glass of water for you."

"Thank you." I offered a smile and waited until Vincent was out of sight before slipping out the side door.

There was nothing like a warm breeze on a warm day to make you feel warmer yet. Stagnate air greeted me as I walked outside. I brushed hair from my eyes as I looked to the right, then to the left. The man was nowhere to be seen. I walked toward the grassy area to my left when my vision blurred. I lost my balance and staggered, tripping over the curb and falling into a family grave marker. I braced myself against the hunk of granite, pulling in deep breaths in an attempt to regain control of my senses. But no matter how much I focused on reigning in my hunting senses, everything was still blurred and distorted around me, as if I were looking through concave glass. Tall statues appeared wide in the middle and soared into the air as if reflected in a funhouse mirror. Headstones flush with the ground were nothing more than colored blobs. And then just like that, I snapped out of it. It took me a moment to realize I hadn't slipped into hunting mode; rather, I had had a vision of my most recent dream. I looked up, trying to process what had happened, when I spotted him.

"Hey," I shouted. I trotted, as much as one could trot in stilettos, toward him but he vanished into thin air. "Oh come on," I muttered.

I quickened my pace and arrived at the spot where he had stood seconds ago, peering around the grave markers. It took a moment, but I spotted him standing partially hidden behind a monument fifty feet away. "Who are you?"

No response. He vanished again.

Slipping off my shoes and grabbing them by the straps, I zigzagged through rows of headstones. When I got to the monument where he had stood, I spotted him another thirty feet away. "What do you want?" He smiled and ducked behind the large base of the statue. My vampire abilities kicked into high gear, and I arrived at the statue a split second later. "What in the hell," I muttered. I was glad he found this game of cat and mouse amusing. I sure didn't. I circled the statue, dragging my hand along the rough base. I stopped and contemplated the absurdity of what I was doing. I didn't know who this vampire was or why he captivated me to the point I felt compelled to follow him around the cemetery. What was I doing? What did I think was going to come of this?

The breeze picked up and knocked acorns from a nearby oak tree. I looked up at the towering tree, its trunk several feet wide. I imagined the tree had been around for hundreds of years. I took note of the statue whose base I stood by. It was an angel with wings almost as long as its body, one hand extended in the air. "Whoa, whoa, whoa," I muttered. I cupped my hands to shield my eyes from the sun and get a better look. My dream flashed across my mind. This was the statue I had dreamt about. Surveying the area, I noted the grid of headstones. Some were exquisite statues, others much shorter, and others flush with the ground and in a variety of colors. These were the objects I previously couldn't discern in my dream.

But unlike my dream, this statue wasn't moving; it wasn't looking at me and pointing in any specific direction. "What are you trying to tell me?" I asked the statue. I closed my eyes in order to pull my dream's vision to the forefront of my mind's eye. In my dream, I had started to walk away when the angel began stomping as a way to catch my attention. And it had worked. So I opened my eyes and started walking, but nothing happened. When I looked back, the angel was still holding its pose, open palm facing the sky.

I recalled the dream again and the direction the angel had pointed. I was too wrapped up in my thoughts to take notice of mist swirling around my ankles. I assessed my surroundings and determined that whatever the statue had wanted me to see in my dream was now somewhere in the direction behind me. I turned on my heels and was faced with a transparent wall of mist that materialized into the vampire I had followed out here.

We stared at each other, taking in one another. There was a familiarity about this vampire, but I couldn't place it. I didn't recall him having attended last year's Halloween party and wasn't sure if I'd come across him in the months after I'd fled and attempted vampire life on my own. He looked at me with squinted eyes and pursed mouth as if studying me and trying to figure out who I was. It was apparent he wasn't going to say anything so I spoke.

"Do I know you?"

His eyes stopped scanning my face and locked with mine. He moved closer, sniffing me, then retreated. Without breaking his stare, he reached inside his jacket, pulled out a piece of paper and handed it to me. I looked at it and then back at him.

"What is this?"

He didn't respond and didn't move; he kept his hand extended holding the piece of paper.

"I don't take things from strangers." I hoped that would get him to talk.

It didn't work. He pushed the paper closer to me.

I glanced at the paper and plucked it from his grasp. It was folded over twice into a small square. I unfolded the paper and read its contents.

"I don't understand," I said. But when I looked up, the vampire was gone. A trail of mist dissipated into the air like fog burning off in the morning sun.

I looked at the message–U.L.E.E.–but didn't know what to make of the initials.

"Allison?" Vincent called out from several yards behind me.

The unexpected sound of his voice startled me. I folded the paper and slipped it into my bra before turning around.

"What are you doing out here?" He looked beyond me, his eyes flitting back and forth as if searching for the reason I had wandered out here.

"I told you I needed air."

"You said you needed water."

"Yes, water and air." I grabbed the bottle of water Vincent extended toward me, twisted the cap and sipped.

"You couldn't get air closer to the chapel?"

"I don't know, Vincent." I threw my hands in the air. "I started wandering and ended up out here. With Felix's funeral and recalling my parents' services which seem like they were just yesterday, I don't feel myself today."

"Mmm," Vincent purred. He stared at me intently, as if examining me, like he was waiting for me to break under the pressure of his glare and confess my sins.

"Well, um, shall we?" I held my hand out in the direction of the chapel.

Instead of accepting, Vincent eyed the angel statue. "So you just so happened to wander out here? To this statue?"

I looked up and feigned ignorance. "Mmm hmm."

"An angel with wings as big as its body with its arms raised to the heavens. This is a coincidence?"

"I know what you're getting at Vincent, and no, this isn't the statue I've dreamt about," I lied.

"Are you sure? I mean it seems odd that you randomly wandered all the way out here," he extended his arms for dramatic effect, "to a statue resembling the exact description of the one in your dream."

"Vincent, I'm the one who saw the statue. It's my dream. And I'm telling you this isn't it. Why would I lie to you, especially after all of the help you've provided in trying to interpret my dream?"

"Well you could let me see your dream so I would know what exactly we're looking for."

"You've asked for that before and you know how I feel about you seeing what's in my dream."

"I told you I would only witness, I wouldn't alter your memories."

"Trust has to be earned; it's not given."

"Mmm. That it is."

Before he could say anything else, the chapel's bell sounded a different toll, indicating the service was about to start.

"Shall we?" I asked again.

Chapter 7

Following the semi-formal chapel service, the congregation gathered around the aboveground sarcophagus in which Felix's coffin had been placed. The ornately carved lid lay off to the side and would be set in place once the service was over and the mourners gone. A minister read from a burial service book and referenced several Bible passages Felix had requested. Most of what the minister was saying was background noise as my mind was otherwise consumed with the cryptic note I had received from the mysterious vampire who was notably absent from this portion of the service.

My attention piqued as the minister quoted: "From the Book of Ezekiel, Chapter 28, Verse 18. By all your sin, even by your evil trading, you have made your holy places unclean; so I will make a fire come out from you, it will make a meal of you, and I will make you as dust on the earth before the eyes of all who see you."

How apropos, I thought.

We concluded by reciting the Lord's Prayer. A mortal assistant then handed each of Felix's siblings a rose, and then handed one to me. Lorenzo blinked incessantly as he attempted to hold back tears. He escorted a weeping Marlo to the casket where they simultaneously laid their roses. Max stood and straightened his jacket, refusing to make eye contact with anyone as he paid his final respect and then walked straight to the limo. Vincent stood and extended his hand to me. I did a double take as I swore I saw Vincent dabbing the corner of his eye. I accepted his gesture and walked with him to the grave.

Clouds reflected on the coffin as a shadow of a buzzard flying high above skimmed over us. Touching the casket with my left hand, I raised the rose in my right hand to my lips and kissed it before placing the bloom on top of the coffin. "Goodbye Felix. We'll find who did this to you." I whispered in a low tone so only Vincent could hear.

"And we'll make them pay, brother," Vincent added.

We looked at each other and exchanged tentative smiles. We were joined in this mission, bound and determined to discover who had done this to Felix. Vincent's fervor for finding the murderer was attractive. There was a sparkle in his eye as he committed to making the perpetrator pay, and I found that oh so sexy. It made me feel things I shouldn't have been feeling at a funeral.

I looked away. I had to. Vincent deserved better. He deserved better than the way I was treating him. One minute I was eager to hop in bed with him, the next I was ready to toss him away like yesterday's paper. But I couldn't give him what he wanted. I couldn't give him my heart.

Vincent gently pulled my arm. I looked over my shoulder. The mourners were waiting for us to pass before paying their final respects.

We walked hand in hand between above ground tombs. In a desperate effort to put the funeral behind me, I distracted my mind by looking for the mystery vampire. I didn't see him, but someone else, or rather two someone-elses, caught my attention.

"What are they doing here?" I hissed and jutted my chin in the direction where Caz sat on a tomb, legs hanging over the side, and Delilah stood, hip resting on the same grave.

Vincent's face turned fifty shades paler than usual. He gulped. "I, uh, I haven't the slightest idea. I thought they'd both fled for good after the altercation with the gypsies."

"I didn't think we'd ever see their faces again given their fearless leader Lucious is trapped in the Garden of Eden."

A low growl escaped Vincent's chest.

"Seems a little suspicious that they show up here, now, don't you agree?" I asked.

"Indeed. Why don't we go over there and ask them."

Vincent walked ahead, and I allowed our hand holding to break. He turned and looked at me. "Allison, what is it? What's wrong?"

"Can you take care of talking to them? I'd like to go home."

Vincent's eyes narrowed. "I won't let them harm you. There's no need to be afraid."

I chuckled. "Without Jal to cast a spell, I'm not really worried about those two. It's just, um, it's been a long day, and my head is pounding."

"But what about the reception? You must thank all of these people for showing their respect today."

"I'm not in the mood to converse with guests, and besides, I don't know most of them anyway."

"I could introduce you."

I bet you could… introduce me as your significant other, I thought. "It has been a trying day, Vincent. I'd like to go home and unwind."

"Does this have anything to do with the statue you were standing next to earlier?"

"Wow, honestly, Vincent? I already told you that wasn't the statue from my dream. Between Felix's funeral and the memory of my parents, and knowing we need to gear up for the search for Felix's killer, I'd simply like to get some rest."

Vincent brushed the back of his hand across my cheek. My eyes met his gaze as I nonverbally tried to convince him of my intentions. "Rest is good. Go. Rest. I'll be over later to help you–help us–unwind." His eyebrow arched provocatively.

I literally bit my tongue. Here we had just left his brother's funeral and he was already suggesting we spend the night together. I wanted the time to study Felix's note and the clue I had received to determine what it might mean to Felix's death or the research he had been doing on me. But I knew if I didn't respond in the affirmative, I'd raise Vincent's suspicions more than they were already, and I couldn't afford that with all of the sleuthing I'd be doing in the coming days.

"Yeah, sure. That'd be great."

Vincent kissed my forehead. "I'll have a private car take you home."

"Thanks," I whispered.

I savored the feel of the cushy leather seat beneath me as I sat in the back of a chauffeured Cadillac. I'd been on my feet for hours, and the effects of four-inch stilettos were loud and clear to my aching calves. My feet were also numb, but not as much as my mind.

For the life of me, I couldn't figure out why Caz and Delilah would return to this area, let alone show up at Felix's funeral. After the shenanigans on Rattlesnake Island this past March, I thought the message was clear they needed to leave—permanently—or risk punishment for collaborating with Jal, the son of a gypsy elder, to open a portal to the Garden of Eden in which Lucious was able to pass through. The thought of Lucious discovering he wasn't alone in the Garden brought a smile to my face. I wondered how he had reacted when he saw Cain, his creator, for the first time in over two million years. But what I really wondered was what was so important that Caz and Delilah would put their lives on the line and return in such a public manner.

The piece of paper wedged in my bra pinched my skin. I pulled out the note, unfolded the paper and stared at the message, wracking my brain for words representing the four individual letters. And then it hit me like a ton of bricks. As I realized what I was looking at, my body tingled as if I'd touched an electric-charged fence. U.L.E.E. weren't initials for four words–it was one word, a name actually, that for whatever reason was written to appear as if the letters represented words for a four-letter phrase.

Very clever, I thought. If my first instinct was that the initials represented four words that together formed a phrase, anyone who might have intercepted the note would have probably been misled as well. This was a coded message.

Ulee was the name of my favorite childhood stuffed animal. It was a unicorn, maybe about a foot tall, with light brown hooves, dark brown eyes and a yellow twisted horn. Ulee had gone everywhere with me, from visits to my grandparents' house, to slumber parties and grocery shopping excursions. And she had been my security blanket every night; I couldn't fall asleep without her. Over my childhood, her mane and tail had become a tangled mess from all of the adventures we had gone on, from imaginary worlds created in the backyard to treks by the creek on warm summer days.

But more importantly, at least for the situation at hand, Ulee was a code word between my parents and me. My parents had of course taught me to never accept a ride (or anything else for that matter) from a stranger, but stressed if anything had ever happened to them, and if somebody other than them had to pick me up from school or wherever, I wasn't to go with them unless that person knew the code word. It was my parents' way of ensuring I wouldn't accept a ride from anybody, even someone I knew like my grandparents or a family friend, if plans hadn't been arranged in advance.

But what did the code word mean coming from a strange vampire?

Was I to trust him? If that were the case, why didn't he talk to me? Why didn't he just say the word and then tell me what he wanted? Did he want me to go with him, as I would have done if I were a child and someone used the code word? Or did this have something to do with my parents? But if so, what? It's not like my parents were alive, and the stranger with the code word was going to take me to them.

"Oh my God," I whispered.

"Is everything all right, ma'am?" the chauffer asked as he looked at me in the rearview mirror.

My initial reaction was to tell him to turn around and take me back to the cemetery, more specifically to my parents' crypt. But I knew that was too risky. I couldn't risk Vincent seeing me and then questioning why I had returned when I told him I had wanted to go home.

"Everything's fine," I replied.

Forty minutes later, I was home in Ridge Hollow. The driver opened the door and helped me from the vehicle. I thanked him and watched as the car disappeared down the driveway.

I was deep in thought about the coded message and what my parents could possibly have to do with my current situation when a familiar scent snapped me back to reality. The hair on the back of my neck stood up, and a chill ran down my spine. I couldn't recall who, but the scent belonged to someone I'd previously met.

I crouched and scampered to the front porch. My back to the exterior wall, I peeked through the front door window. I didn't see anyone. Clinging to the perimeter of the house, I glanced around the side, and when I confirmed the coast was clear, rounded the corner. I repeated the same steps as I approached the back of the house when I heard footsteps inside. The intruder was in the den.

I slid the key into the backdoor's lock and turned the handle, cautious to not tip off the trespasser. When I entered the house, the person's spicy yet feminine scent surrounded me, filling my nostrils. I slid off my heels and tiptoed around the couch and in the direction of the den when she walked out, book in hand.

"Lucretia?"

Chapter 8

Lucretia was still wearing the same painted-on gray dress she had worn to the funeral. Her knee-length black hair was now pulled back and piled onto the top of her head, the gray streak spiraling through the messy bun.

"Hello, Allison," Lucretia greeted. She spoke confidently, as if she belonged there and I should have been expecting her.

"It was you," I accused. My eyes darted between her face and the book she held open in both hands.

Lucretia shrugged, not confirming what I was referring to but also not denying it.

"Oh, don't give me that look like you don't know what I'm talking about," I hissed. "You're the one who ransacked the library at the Drake's castle."

"I did what?" she coyly asked as she gave me her best pouty face.

I charged past Lucretia and looked in the den. Books had been pulled from the shelves and lay stacked on the desk and floor. "What are you looking for?"

A Cheshire cat grin spread across her face. "Answers."

"Answers to what? What do you think you're going to find in these books?"

"You seem to forget, young Allison, that I was with Vincent for centuries. I know he's a historian and that he's recorded the history he's witnessed in these volumes."

"So what, you want a history lesson?"

"No. I said I was searching for answers."

"And you still haven't said which answers to which questions."

Lucretia closed the book and placed it on the end table. She chuckled. "Silly child, I'm looking for answers about you."

"Oh for Pete's sake! You're not over Vincent breaking up with you and moving on with me?"

Lucretia's face drained of all color. I must have hit a nerve. She rolled her head, cracking her neck as she licked her red-glossed lips. "I want to know what makes you so special that Vincent risked his existence to transform you into a vampire without your consent."

"Apparently you didn't pay attention at the last Ruling Council meeting. Felix produced proof of my consent."

"Please. The other seated Council members may have bought that little charade, but I didn't."

"Didn't you authenticate the video?"

"Oh sure, the documentation was tested and of course panned out, but again, that was no surprise either. Who knows what lengths Vincent went to in order to clear his name? Well, not many know, but I have a pretty good idea of how far he'd go and what he's capable of."

I narrowed my eyes as I processed her last statement. "Wait. What are you saying? Are you accusing Vincent of having killed Felix?"

"I'm not saying that at all. I have no idea who killed Felix."

"No, apparently I'm your biggest concern."

Lucretia smiled. She walked into the pantry and emerged with two blood bags. "Care for one of these?" She tossed a bag at me. "I hear this is your new food du jour."

I caught the bag and set it on the table. "Why are you so enamored with me? Is it simple jealousy?"

Lucretia exhaled audibly. Her fangs emerged as she raised the bag to her lips and tore off the top with one attempt. She chugged the liquid, her eyes never leaving me. Throwing the bag on the kitchen counter, she wiped her lips and glared.

"I know Vincent –"

"Yeah," I interrupted. "We've gone over that already.""So rude. If you'd let me finish, I was going to say I know Vincent has a penchant for rare and unique things."

"What's your point?"

"And that penchant also carries over to his lovers."

I gulped. I had first learned of Vincent's proclivity for rare items last year when Marlo had intervened and stopped me from running off with him after the Halloween party. He had been drawn to me since I was the first descendant to show signs of vampirism. No one like me had ever existed before. And that was right up Vincent's alley–just another collectible to add to his ever growing collection of rare cars, castles and artwork. Anyone and everyone who knew Vincent knew this, so it was no surprise to me that Lucretia, having dated Vincent for centuries, also knew this. But this wasn't good. Outwardly, there was nothing exceptional about me so that meant Lucretia was going to keep digging to find out what special gift I possessed that had drawn Vincent to me. No other vampires outside of the Drakes knew my lineage existed; that Cain, after transforming into a vampire, had an affair with a mortal and produced the first half vampire/half mortal child this world had ever seen. And from then on, the Devil's bloodline had been passed down through the generations. If Lucretia kept digging, she was going to find out what exactly made me so special. Heaven only knew what it would mean if that information were public knowledge and what it would mean for other descendants.

"Oh really?" It was my turn to play coy, turning the tables on her. "And what exactly was so special about you that Vincent spent centuries by your side?"

"I'm a seer," she replied without missing a beat.

"A seer? You foretell the future?"

"Indeed I do." She walked to the sofa table and picked up the framed dried rose. "Is this yours?"

"Of course it is; it's in my house. So what exactly did you help Vincent see?" I wanted to feel her out, learn about the sorts of things she had helped Vincent with in order to assess this threat.

She dragged a finger along the table as she walked toward the den, turning before she got there, looking at the wall hangings. She was having a good time with all of this. "Oh you know, I helped him with the little things like taking down powerful empires. Ever hear of the fall of the Roman Empire? Yeah, we orchestrated that. Together we took down world leaders, Hollywood legends and socialites–all because we could. And in doing so we amassed an ungodly amount of wealth… money, jewels, the lost Inca Gold, the Midas Touch… yes, it really does exist."

Oh my God, I thought. I was looking at someone who had drastically altered the course–several courses–of history. And I was sleeping with her partner in crime. If I made it through these next few days, I was going to have to spend some quality time with Vincent's historical accounts. "Let me guess. Vincent left you empty handed, and you're searching for where he hid the treasure so you can reclaim what rightfully belongs to you."

"Good guess, but no. I wouldn't have been so naïve as to have let that happen. With all I was able to give Vincent, there was no reason for him to leave me unless…."

"Unless what?"

"Unless Vincent found someone who could give him something I couldn't." Her heels knocked against the wood floor as she walked over to me, stopping a foot away. "So I'll ask again, Allison. What is it that makes you so valuable to Vincent?" She backed me into the corner. "Hmm?"

"If you're a seer, then why don't you already know the answer to that question?"

Lucretia snorted and backed away. The doorbell rang. Lucretia sniffed the air like a ravenous animal scouting its next meal. "You have an interesting visitor."

I walked through the foyer and peeked out the window. I pulled the door open. "Now's not a good time, Matt."

Matt pushed through the doorway and stopped in the foyer. "I have something to tell you."

"Who is this?" Lucretia inquired from the living room.

Matt looked at her and then back at me. "Who's this?"

I sighed and closed the door. "Matt, Lucretia. Lucretia, Matt."

Matt extended a hand toward Lucretia but I stepped in front of him to prevent the two from touching.

"So Matt," Lucretia spat the 't'. "What brings a knighted archangel to the home of a vampire?"

Both Matt's and my mouth dropped.

"How do you..." Matt started.

"Oh please, I can smell it on you. Not only are the scents of frankincense and myrrh part of your essence since you were born an angel, but the scents are stronger since you've been knighted."

I sniffed the air and only then noticed how much heavier Matt's natural scent was.

"You didn't know that, now did you?" Lucretia raised an eyebrow in my direction. "So tell me, Matt. What did you have to tell Allison that's so important that you came here and risked punishment at the hand of the Army? Boy Allison, you sure have a lot of men in your life willing to risk theirs for you."

"What is she talking about?" Matt whispered to me.

"You don't have to answer anything she asks you, Matt."

The door burst open. Matt and I both turned to see who it was.

I groaned.

Vincent charged in. "I knew it! I knew you were lying when you left the funeral early saying you needed to rest." Vincent stopped in front of me, Matt behind him. Vincent's chest heaved with long, heavy breaths. Without looking at Matt, he asked, "What is *he* doing here?"

I shifted my eyes over Vincent's shoulder. Matt looked like a deer caught in headlights: frozen still, eyes wide, mouth clamped shut.

Vincent whirled around. "You know you aren't supposed to be here." He jabbed Matt in the shoulder. "And you," he pointed a finger at me as he walked into the living room, "know better than to be carrying on with angels. How many times do you need to be warned? The both of you? What's it going to take to get it through your thick skulls that you cannot be carrying on like this?" Vincent stopped ranting when he spotted Lucretia. She waggled her fingers at him. "What in the hell are you doing here?"

"It's one big meeting of the exes," I said.

"Exes?" Lucretia questioned.

"Matt and I are married, I mean were married, I mean he's widowed now that I'm a vampire."

"Interesting," Lucretia mused. "And the plot thickens."

"I'm going to go," Matt said, "so you three vampires can talk, or whatever it is you need to do."

I wanted to plead with Matt not to leave, but figured it would be best to stay quiet in front of my other two unwelcome visitors. Pleading with Matt would only incite Vincent and further intrigue Lucretia. Matt, never turning his back on us, slipped out, closing the door behind him.

"You never answered my question," Vincent poked a finger at Lucretia.

"Let's get something straight, Vincent. I don't have to answer any of your questions. However, since your little girlfriend here knows the reason for my visit, I'm sure she would clue you in sooner or later. I'm on to you. I know you're up to something. You left me for Allison because she can give you something I couldn't, and I'm going to find out what that is. So chew on that."

Vincent opened his mouth but nothing came out. If it weren't for the situation, I'd have found it comical that for once, he was at a loss for words. Lucretia matched his stare, offered a snarky smile, then stormed out of my house, brushing my shoulder as she passed, slamming the door so hard the widows shook in their frames.

I didn't know what to say or do so I waited for Vincent to make the first move. He turned, head still down but eyes focused on me. "What did she want from you?"

"I don't know." Vincent went to interject. I raised my hands. "Honestly, I don't know. She was already here when the driver dropped me off. My guess is that she skipped out of the latter part of the service and came here looking for answers." I motioned my thumb toward the den.

Vincent rushed to the den and surveyed the damage. "She was the one who broke into the castle and destroyed our library."

"That's what I thought too at first, but when I asked her about it, she didn't own up to it, not that I'd expect her to, but she also looked surprised by the accusation."

"No, it was her. It had to have been her. And Matthew? Why was he here?" Red tinted his blue eyes for the briefest of moments.

"I honestly don't know that either, Vincent. He showed up out of the blue, unannounced."

Vincent paced the living room and ran a hand through his hair. "Is anything missing?"

"What?"

"Is anything missing from the house?" he screamed, hands shaking in front of him. "Look around, Allison, it's important."

"Well, I don't know." I scanned the den and living room and then the kitchen. "Well she drank a blood bag."

"No, not that. Is anything belonging to you–a personal effect– missing? Look, Allison!" Veins popped in Vincent's neck.

I frantically scanned the living quarters not knowing what I was looking for. "No, it doesn't look like it. Wait a minute."

"What is it?" Vincent rushed to my side.

"My picture is missing. I had a framed rose right here." I pointed to the sofa table, the exact spot visible as it was the only dust-free area.

"Son of a…." Vincent walked to the table, grabbed the edges and leaned over like he was taking a break after a long run. The veins in his hands popped beneath the surface of his skin, which reddened as he squeezed harder, his knuckles whitening.

"What's wrong? It was only a picture frame with a rose I'd found in one of the books."

Vincent whirled around. "It's not *just* a picture frame," he yelled. I stepped back, shocked by his reaction. "It's how she sees things, Allison." Vincent swept his arm over the table knocking the lamp to the floor. "She needs to hold something belonging to the person she wants to read or see or whatever in the hell it is she does. Do you understand what this means?"

My voice caught in my throat. "Sh… she can see things about me, right?" And then I blurted, "But only of my future? Nothing of my past, so my secret, the fact I'm a descendant and what that means, she can't see, right?"

Vincent paced the room. He clenched his jaw. The muscles in his cheeks and neck flexed. His face flushed. "To an extent, that's right. But who knows what she sees in your future that allows her to connect the dots with whatever she found here in my books or the books at the castle, of your past, of your ancestors' past. This is not good, Allison. Not good at all." He kicked the love seat and grunted like a tennis player who had just whacked a ball.

I watched as he flung pillows and punched the fireplace hard enough to cause some bricks to crumble and crack his knuckles open. I'd never seen Vincent so upset, and I was afraid if I didn't intervene, my house might not survive his wrath.

"Come. Sit." I patted the couch. Vincent huffed and continued mumbling under his breath. I grabbed him by the shoulders and turned him to face me. "Hey, I get it. Lucretia now possesses something of mine and is able to see things about me. I don't want that intrusion in my life. So we'll get it back.""What?" Vincent looked at me, face twisted, like I was crazy.

"We'll get the picture back. Once we've reclaimed what's mine, she'll no longer be able to see my future, right?"

"It won't be easy, Allison. When that woman has her mind set on something, it's very hard to change it. She'll guard the picture with her life. It's the only way she can see things about you, and it allows her to still stay connected to me. You saw her before. Do you honestly think she's going to let us get close to the frame?" Vincent grabbed the recliner and flung it across the floor, the rubber feet leaving black skid marks on the wood.

"Hey, hey, hey, there's no sense in taking your frustration out on the furniture. We know the damage that's been done, and we'll fix it." I pulled Vincent down to the couch. He gasped as he regained control of his breath. He cracked his knuckles, the cuts already healed, dried blood left behind. "So why don't we take our minds off of this."

Vincent raised his eyebrows. He inhaled a few more times, his eyes combing my face. "What did you have in mind?"

I smiled and ran my hand through his hair, trying to build the courage to offer something I didn't want to offer, but doing what I knew was the only thing that would settle him. "Stay here with me tonight."

Chapter 9

A chill ran over my body as the morning breeze caressed my skin, cooling it from the blazing inferno it had been only a few hours ago. I yanked the sheet, barely able to muster a small corner of fabric to cover my midsection. I shivered and was instantly reminded why I couldn't warm up this morning–Vincent. I didn't have to look to know he was entwined with the sheets and hogging the fabric.

It was too early in the morning to allow my temper to flare so I focused on the chirping birds, hoping their melody would allow my mind to escape. The breeze blew again, rattling tree leaves and billowing the drapes into the room. I sucked in a lung-full of the clean air, relishing the scent of the last bit of summer as fall slowly made its appearance. I held my breath as I peeked with one eye. The curtains settled, leaving a gap, allowing sunlight to filter into the room. A line of light cast on my pillow only a few inches from my face. I placed my hand on the pillow and slid my index finger toward the light. Warmth greeted my nail first, then the rest of my finger. I watched, knowing the sunlight wouldn't cause me to burst into flames, but waiting for the pain I knew would come. After about a minute, the sun had sufficiently agitated the venom in my system. Bubbles percolated beneath the surface of my skin. I pulled my hand to my chest and rubbed my finger. Rolling onto my back, I glanced at Vincent, whose back was facing me. I exhaled, expelling all air from my lungs and attempted to expunge all memories of last night. I was upset with myself. I had complete control over the creator's bond, something I wasn't sure Vincent was fully aware of, or if he was, he had chosen to ignore it. Last night's rendezvous couldn't be blamed on the bond. I only had myself to fault. Spending the night with Vincent was the only thing I could think of to calm him from his Lucretia-induced rage. The alternative wouldn't have been viable–me telling Vincent to leave once again. He mentally couldn't have handled that last night. At least not handled it well. So I did what I had thought best.

I wasn't proud of what I'd done. All physical gratification I felt last night was wiped out by the remorse I felt this morning. I was lying to myself and lying to Vincent. Last night, as his lips met mine and consumed me with a kiss, my mind was elsewhere. I thought of Matt. As Vincent's hands ran up my shirt, I thought about the way Matt used to touch me. As Vincent chased me upstairs to the bedroom, I had flashbacks of Matt chasing me around our home in Buzzard Hill. The thoughts were too much to handle. I wanted–desperately–to be with Matt, but here I was with Vincent. I rationalized, as much as I could between passionate kisses, that Matt and I couldn't be together given I was a vampire and he an angel, so why should I starve myself of my physical needs? And with that, I let the need for physical contact devour my mind and drown out all thoughts of Matt, banishing his image to the black, murky depths of my mind. Yet here I was the next morning, thinking–again–about Matt, the man I couldn't have.

I sat up and steadied myself from falling over. Black and white dots invaded my vision. I rubbed my eyes before pushing myself off of the bed and once again stumbling back. At first, I chalked it up to moving too quickly first thing in the morning, but then felt the thumping, burning pain of a vampire bite. I raised a hand to my neck and touched the bite wounds Vincent had inflicted during our escapade. It wasn't uncommon for him to do this; in fact we both bit each other during our dalliances. Having another vampire's blood in your system while experiencing physical pleasure heightened the experience on an emotional and physical level. It was like riding the adrenaline rush from driving a racecar, but then kicking it up a notch by flipping the NOS switch. It was more addictive than human blood. But this wound felt too fresh. He had bitten me late at night and I should have healed by now. I stumbled to the dresser and picked up the mirror. The two marks were still pink. A trail of dried blood caked on my neck. I was going to have to talk to Vincent about this. It was one thing to take a little nip, but quite another when he drained me and left me this weak. Then I corrected my thinking. There was a lot more I had to discuss with Vincent. I needed to break things off with him.

I washed up, changed clothes and downed a couple of blood bags. The cool liquid was what the doctor had ordered. The bite marks healed as I ingested the nourishment, the skin on my neck tightening, the burning gone. The shakes dissipated as I gained strength, and within a few minutes, I felt like my usual self. Well, almost.

I grabbed my phone and texted Matt, asking him to meet me at my parents' crypt. I promised him there would be no unwanted visitors and I'd explain everything that happened yesterday. I went to the garage and looked at my Vette, but decided I was in the mood for a run.

It had taken me all of about ten minutes to arrive at the cemetery, significantly faster than the 45-minute car ride, but running might not have been the best decision. As I skidded to a halt, I felt lightheaded, and spots danced across my vision. I grabbed a tree trunk for support as I bent over to catch my breath. Maybe I should have had another blood bag or two before I left the house.

After regaining my composure, I checked my phone for a response from Matt, but there was none. Maybe he hadn't received my message yet. I circled the stone crypt as I waited, impulsively checking my phone what seemed like every two minutes. A hunger pain pierced my stomach, and heat clawed its way up my throat. My arms crossed my midsection, and I hunched over. "No, no, no," I whispered as I attempted to will-away my hunger. Venom began churning in my belly, confirming my earlier thought that I should have drank more blood before coming here. I squeezed my eyes shut, focusing all of my energy on the hunger pains, envisioning I was placing them in a box, closing the lid, and putting the box in storage to be opened another day. After tucking the vision away, I slowly opened my eyes, waiting for another angry growl. If that were to happen, I was prepared to refocus and suppress the urge as Max had taught me. There was no growl. I gave myself a mental pat on the back for accomplishing that on my first attempt.

Still crouched, I lifted my head, looking up at the crypt. I focused on the inscription, Kane, etched into the stone placard. The plan had been to eventually hyphenate Carmichael after my maiden name once this became the final resting spot for me and my husband.

"Ali?"

I flinched at the sound of Matt's voice. "You came?" I stood and turned, intending to greet him, but stopped as I walked into a wall of his scent. My stomach growled, the venom awakening. I clutched my stomach and held my breath, hoping that by not breathing, the venom would go back to sleep.

Matt eyed me suspiciously. "You seem surprised I came."

"After yesterday, I wasn't sure if you'd ever come around again."

"Yeah, nice friends you keep," Matt joked. "Who was the lady?"

"Ugh." I rolled my eyes. "Lucretia, Vincent's jilted ex-lover."

"What was Vincent's ex doing at your house?"

"Trust me, she wasn't invited."

"What about Vincent?" Matt's voice changed, going cold as Vincent's name rolled off of his tongue. "What was he doing there?"

His change in tone momentarily stole my voice. "Matthew Carmichael, is that a twinge of jealousy I hear?"

"Jealousy? Why would I be jealous? We're no longer married. You can see whomever you want."

I pursed my lips and looked at him like a teacher scolding a child, telling him without saying a word that I wasn't buying what he was selling.

"Are you two together? Dating?" Matt asked.

"So you won't answer my questions about the chick at your house the other day, but you expect me to answer your questions about my relationship status?" I sat down on the marble entrance to the tomb. The lightheadedness was back. I stole a quick gulp of air and rubbed my eyes.

"Hey, are you okay?" Matt asked. He took a few steps toward me but I held up my hand to stop him. I didn't want him to get too close as I didn't trust myself around him at the moment with my flaring appetite.

I rubbed my neck. "I'm fine. Just a little weak."

"Here," Matt held out his wrist.

I looked at it inquisitively and then up at his hazel eyes. "What are you doing?"

"You're hungry, right? That's why you're weak. You need blood, don't you?"

I stood and walked away. I needed more fresh air, not air tainted with the sweet smell of Matt's essence. "Really, Matt? Give me some credit. My urge for human blood is under control. You know that."

"Sorry, I was only trying to help."

"Waving a vein in front of a recovering blood addict isn't help." I threw him a stern look.

"Sorry." Matt looked away sheepishly. After a few moments he asked, "Why'd you do it?"

"Do what?"

"Why'd you become a vampire, Ali?"

"Why did I *become* a vampire? Did you really just ask me that?"

Matt nodded.

"Matt, you remember the symptoms I had–lack of appetite, insomnia, infertility–all of the seemingly common ailments that doctors couldn't diagnose. I didn't choose this. It chose me. It was in my blood."

"Yeah, but Gabriela said that even if you were a descendant with symptoms of vampirism, you still had to consent to your transformation. So why did you consent?"

I sighed. "This isn't why I asked you to meet me here."

Matt didn't respond. He looked away. As much as I didn't want to talk about this, it was obvious he had questions. And I had the answers. I supposed the least I could do was answer his questions honestly.

"I don't know, Matt, okay? I don't know. I don't even remember consenting but Felix had video from that night. You couldn't see anything because the camera had been knocked over, but you could clearly hear I gave Vincent permission to change me. That night was a blur, Matt. My symptoms were accelerating. I almost attacked Jenna because I couldn't control myself. I wasn't myself that night. I certainly don't remember consenting, but how do you argue with video that was taken in the room at the time it happened?" Tears welled in my eyes. "I didn't want this, Matt."

"I'm sorry for asking, Ali. I had no idea. I just wondered how you could... if it was easy for you to do... or...."

I waved him off and took another breath, blowing air out of my mouth to prevent tears from falling.

"Since we're playing 50 questions here, it's my turn. After the car accident, why didn't you come looking for me?" Matt's mouth fell open. I raised an eyebrow waiting for his response. "Vincent returned you to our home, your memory intact. Didn't you wonder what had happened to me?"

"Of course I wondered about you, Ali," Matt responded defensively. "But before I even had five minutes to think about what had happened, Gabriela was in my face giving me a history lesson about my angel lineage, filling me in on the existence of vampires, informing me that I was now an official member of Saint Michael's Army and then whisked me off to archangel boot camp."

"Archangel boot camp?"

"Seriously. That shit was the real deal – physical training, more history lessons, sword training, learning to fly, brainwashing me in an attempt to get over you. They kept me busy on purpose, to keep me distracted from searching for you. Ali, if I had had it my way, I would have taken off looking for you as soon as Vincent dumped me on my doorstep. But Gabriela and her posse were waiting for me and they definitely had a plan."

"Are you?"

Matt shook his head. "Am I what?"

"Are you over me? You said they brainwashed you to try to get over me."

"Ali, no, but things are different now. We can't–"

I waved my hands, cutting him off. I didn't want to hear again how we couldn't be together. "Matt, it's okay, you don't have to explain yourself."

Matt cleared his throat. "So, uh, why did you want to meet here?"

He looked at the crypt. "It isn't every day you get a text telling you to meet someone at the cemetery."

"I received a clue that leads me to believe whoever sent it wanted me to come here."

"Felix's letter? But how did you tie that message to your parent's tomb?"

"No, not that letter. Yesterday, at Felix's funeral, some strange man–a vampire–appeared and gave me this note." I handed the folded paper to Matt.

"A mysterious man hands you a note that reads U.L.E.E. and you think it has something to do with your parents?"

"I know. It sounds a little far-fetched. Do you know what the note means?"

"I'm sorry. If this is the reason you called me here, I can't help."

"Remember my stuffed unicorn? It was my favorite childhood toy. After we were married, I still couldn't part with it and she sat up on a shelf at the top of my closet."

"Yeah, I remember."

"Her name was Ulee."

"Okay, and that means what for purposes of this letter?"

"Not only was Ulee my stuffed animal's name, it was also a secret code word between my parents and me."

"Secret code word for what?"

"In the event my parents couldn't pick me up from school or somewhere else, I wasn't supposed to go with anyone unless they gave me the code word. That way I'd be assured my parents had talked to that person, and they had given them authority to pick me up. And the word was to give me peace of mind I was going with someone my parents trusted."

Matt perked up. "Did anyone else know the word?"

"No, that's the point, Matt. Only the three of us knew the word, and honestly, I hadn't thought about this in years given that it was from my childhood."

"So how did this stranger know the word?"

"I don't know. I could only deduce that by him having the code word, it's safe for me to trust him, or it was a message telling me to come here."

"Since the person who knew the code word would take you back to your parents?"

"Yes, exactly. Plus, when the mystery vampire showed up at the funeral, he led me into the cemetery to a statue resembling the one in my dream. Once at the statue, I realized the direction it had been pointing to in my dream, and it was in the direction of this crypt. That can't be a coincidence."

"No, I don't think it is. So are we supposed to wait around for him to show up?"

"I don't think that would be a good use of our time given the note didn't indicate a date or time or anything."

"Yeah, you're right. So do you think there's another clue here?" Matt walked around the structure, studying it from top to bottom. "If so, I don't know where someone would have left it." He arrived back at the front and stopped in his tracks when he saw my hands on the chains that secured the metal gates and the wood doors behind. "You have to be kidding me."

"Nope, not kidding you."

"You think a clue is inside?"

"Not sure, but there's only way to find out."

"But Ali, that lock is old. If someone would have broken in here, wouldn't you expect to see a new lock?"

I wiggled the rusty lock, the size of my palm. "We're dealing with vampires here. Who knows what we should or shouldn't expect."

"How are we going to get inside? Do you know how to pick a lock?"

I smiled, realizing Matt hadn't witnessed all of my vampire abilities. I yanked on the chain and it snapped like a twig underfoot.

"Whoa." Matt squeezed my arm. "That little bicep packs that much power? I suppose you won't have any issues opening these doors then." Matt twisted the doorknob and threw himself into the wooden doors, but they didn't budge.

"Step back," I said. When Matt was far enough away to not get hurt by flying debris, I donkey kicked the door, sending the doors swinging on their hinges. "Vampirism has its privileges."

"Impressive," Matt remarked, offering a soft smile as he walked into the family mausoleum.

The crypt's narrow entryway was cool and dusty. A few steps in and we were in a larger room where my parents' sarcophaguses rested. Cobwebs had collected on the sills of the leaded glass windows. Sunlight filtered through the stained glass, dust particles sparkling in the light. Dad's tomb was all the way to the left, and my mother's tomb was to his right. There were two empty pyres intended for Matt and me once our days here on earth were past.

"I remember your parents like they were here yesterday," Matt said.

"I know, right?" My fingers combed over the engraving in the wall of my parents' names and dates of birth and death. "It's hard to believe they've been gone seven years."

"You know I still think about them?"

"You do?" I whirled around and faced Matt. He was closer to me than I had expected, and I almost fell into him. I took another quick breath and held it.

"Yeah, Ali, I do. They were good to me. After my parents' deaths, your parents were like parents to me. They treated me like their son."

The sentiment made me smile. "Well they did love you, Mr. Carmichael." I playfully walked my fingers over Matt's chest and he caught my wrist. "You were everything they wanted in a partner for their baby girl." We stood and gazed at each other. Butterflies fluttered in my stomach, as they'd always had when I looked into those eyes. The corner of my mouth turned up and quivered, making Matt smile. Our eyes combed over each other's faces. I took a tiny step forward and leaned toward Matt when he dropped my wrist to sneeze into the crook of his arm.

Internally, I sighed. I wanted those delicious lips on mine, to feel the warmth of his mouth after all these months. "God bless you," I said and turned away to hide my disappointment.

"Ugh, thanks. Too much dust in here for me. So um, what exactly are we looking for again? There's not much in here, not many places to hide a clue."

"You're right about that," I said.

Matt walked the perimeter of the room looking for a loose stone that may have concealed something. I approached the sarcophaguses and examined the ornate scrollwork etched into the lids. I set my hand on my mom's tomb and bent over to get a better view of the side. When I stood eye level with the top, I noticed it. A note tucked under the dried bouquet of roses I had set on top the day of my mom's funeral.

"Matt, I think I found something."

I pulled the envelope from under the browned petals that had a hint of pink left to them.

"What is it?" I held up the envelope which was the size and shape of ones commonly delivered with a floral arrangement.

"It's a note. I found it under the flowers, and I did not leave a note when we buried mom. If I had, this would be coated in seven years' worth of dust and it's not."

"Open it. What does it say?"

I shoved my finger under the flap before pausing at the sight of the wax seal. I tore open the envelope and in the process cut myself. "Ouch," I quipped. I instinctively put the finger in my mouth and when I pulled it out, the cut was healed. Matt's eyes went wide at the sight of my self-healing powers. I smiled.

"Boy, vampirism sure does have its privileges," he nodded.

Pulling out the note, I unfolded it and read it three times.

"What does it say, Ali?"

"Not much. *'A clue lies in your family tree.'*" I flipped the card over for Matt to see.

Matt repeated the clue after grabbing the paper from my hands and reading it.

"Matt, this doesn't tell us anything we don't already know. The clue in my family tree is that I'm one of Cain's descendants. Ugh," I growled.

"Who did the letter come from? Maybe that person doesn't know that you know."

"It's from Felix," I said and flipped the envelope over. "This is his seal."

Matt pondered for a moment, pulling the card to his face, brow furrowed.

"What is it?" I asked.

"There's something here," Matt said.

"What is it?"

"It's faintly written, almost as if Felix's hand smudged the pencil markings. Look in the upper right hand corner. Felix didn't use any dashes or anything between the numbers for month, day and year. Based on this, he wrote this note two weeks ago. I thought at first maybe he had written it before you knew you were a descendant, but this proves otherwise. There has to be something else in your family tree, Ali. Felix was aware that you knew you were a descendant. The note can't possibly allude to that especially if he recently wrote this."

I snatched the note back from Matt and observed the date. "You're right, Matt. But what could it be referring to? What else could be in my family tree?"

"I don't know. But I think it's time we start taking matters into our own hands instead of standing around waiting for clues to appear. What else do you know about your family?"

I exhaled and blew my bangs up in the air. "Just that the venom was passed down on my mother's side of the family."

A loud thud came from the roof followed by scampering as whoever, or whatever, hit the roof was trying to gain traction. Matt and I looked at each before bolting for the door.

Once outside, I scoured the surrounding area. I didn't see anyone, but I certainly smelled what was becoming an all too familiar scent. "Lucretia," I seethed.

Matt stopped behind me. "Did you say Lucretia? As in Vincent's ex, Lucretia?"

"Yes." I paced as I unsuccessfully scanned the grounds for her.

"What is she doing here?"

I ignored Matt's question and instead closed my eyes. Taking deep breaths, I relaxed. My ears welcomed sounds they couldn't hear outside of hunting mode. I couldn't relish the new sounds as time was of the essence. I opened my eyes. My vision cut through the sea of monuments and trees. To the north, I spotted the freeway, to the south, a residential neighborhood. Looking east, I saw Lucretia as she vaulted over the wrought iron fence and fled.

"Allison?" Matt said as he grabbed my shoulder. "Oh my God, Ali.

What's going on with you?"

Matt's voice was like an unexpected footstep for a predator in the woods skulking prey. I redirected my attention to him. His features were a blur, but his pumping heart and coursing blood were clearly visible. One whiff of his fragrance was all the venom needed.

I lunged, the sight of Matt's beating heart and blood pulsing through his veins too much for a hungry vampire, especially one on the hunt. At the same time, there was a flash, and an outline of wings appeared in my distorted vision. Another breath and that sweet scent filled my nose and struck a nerve. It dawned on me who was with me—Matt.

I pulled in my hunting senses. "Oh my God, Matt, I'm so sorry. You know I'd never hurt you."

Matt stood, his wings flapping behind him, an arm over his shoulder ready to unsheathe his sword. "And I never want to hurt you either, but that was a little too close for my liking."

"I'm sorry, Matt," I pleaded. "I engaged my hunting senses so I could hear and see farther. I was only trying to find Lucretia, I swear it."

Matt's wings receded into his back. "Yeah, well, um, I had better go."

"No, wait." I grabbed Matt's arm and turned him around. "Please, I need help. Something is amiss, and I don't think I can do this on my own."

Matt narrowed his eyes. "What do you think is going on?"

"I don't know, Matt. Lucretia is trying to figure out Vincent's end game. She said as much yesterday when she was at my house. You see, she's a seer—"

"You mean she can see the future?" He chuckled in disbelief.

"Yeah, sort of. She needs to be in possession of an object belonging to the person whose future she wants to see. She and Vincent together, they'd used her ability to take down empires and stuff like that. They were together for centuries, so she knows him quite well and is convinced there must be something special about me if Vincent left her and her seeing abilities for me. I mean she's obviously following me. And Vincent. Well he's watching my every move. I can barely do anything on my own without him questioning what I did and whom I was doing it with. And then couple all that with Felix's cryptic message. Matt, something is going on. There's more to all of this than what meets the eye."

"I agree with you about that."

"You do?" Matt's sudden about face in attitude took me off guard.

"The reason I stopped at your house yesterday was because I discovered something. Something I think you'll find quite interesting."

"What is it?"

"It's about the wooden bullets."

"What about them?" My heart skipped a beat as my mind raced with ideas about what Matt was going to say.

Matt grabbed my hand and inspected my scarred thumb. "Can you see that?"

I pulled my hand closer to my face for inspection. "See what? It's a scar."

"You can't see the inscription from the bullet because it's only visible to angels. Archangels to be exact."

My blood pressure skyrocketed. I didn't think I was going to like what I assumed I was about to hear. "Are you telling me an angel killed Felix?"

"No, Ali, I don't know who killed Felix, but I do know he was killed with a bullet belonging to Saint Michael's Army." I objected but Matt cut me off. "Hear me out."

"Fine," I said, crossing my arms over my chest.

"Since becoming fully knighted in Saint Michael's Army, I'm privy to more information than your average angel."

"Yeah? What kind of information, Matt?"

"There are monthly meetings with our flock, all of our flock including the highest ranking members. The purpose of these meetings is to discuss interventions we've had over the past month and to share information on hits we've heard about or where our services are needed. But there's also a session where we talk about weapons in our war to save human souls." Matt paused; I said nothing. "I was in a sidebar conversation, and one of my peers mentioned he'd heard about wooden bullets that had been crafted out of the wood from the cross used at Jesus' crucifixion. At Saint Michael's request, the Lord supposedly sanctioned the use of the wood, the ultimate symbol of God's sacrifice for mankind, when the Army was first formed. Allison, those wooden bullets, only those crafted from the cross on which Jesus hung, can kill a vampire."

There was a long pause.

"Say something, Ali."

"I'm stunned. I don't know what to say. How long have you known about these bullets?"

"I've known about them for some time—"

"You denied any knowledge of those bullets when we met yesterday."

"That's because I needed to be sure."

"Be sure of what exactly?"

"When I was at your house yesterday, and you showed me your thumb, I saw the inscription: *Quis ut Deus?* that was burned into your flesh after you touched the wooden bullet."

"What does it mean?"

"It's the inscription on Saint Michael's shield. It means 'Who is like God?'"

"And why are you telling me this now instead of yesterday?"

"Given I had never seen one of these bullets—I'd only heard hearsay and rumor—I needed to verify for myself what one looked like."

"And did you? Did you verify that?"

"I did. I snuck into the basement of Saint John's Cathedral."

"The cathedral in downtown Cleveland?"

"Yes, that's where the Army meets and where we store a cache of weapons."

"You have a cache of weapons stashed in the basement of a house of worship?"

"Yes, Ali. I know how that sounds."

"Weapons intended to kill sanctioned by an establishment that preaches love and acceptance. It sounds hypocritical."

"Ali—"

"I know, I know," I waved my hand. "Vampires versus angels. It's a whole different ballgame. But you said you found the bullets, right?"

"Yeah, but it wasn't easy."

"What do you mean?"

"All of our weapons are secured to ensure they don't fall into the wrong hands. But these bullets were stored in a separate room, one requiring a different access pass than the one I have. I managed to get into the room and found the bullets stored in an air-tight case, under a glass encasement like you'd see in a museum, with an alarm."

"How'd you get into the room?"

"I uh, 'borrowed' Gabriela's card key."

"You what? By borrow, I assume you mean you took it without her permission. Does she know?"

"I don't think so."

"And triple security—alarm, glass and a case. Why?"

"I don't know."

"So you weren't able to touch the bullets?"

"No, I didn't have the code to disarm the security system, but I was able to see the inscription and it was on every bullet in the case."

"Who has the code?"

"I'm guessing only a select few commanders. But I don't know. I mean the most anyone has heard about these bullets is through rumors."

"If Gabriela has a key card gaining her access to that room, would she have the security code for the alarm?"

"I don't know. I mean I guess. But I don't want to jump to any conclusions."

"Why so nervous?" Matt looked at me before looking away. "Matt, what is it?"

"The case that held the bullets, I could tell it was made for that specific purpose. It was a wooden box with a red silk lining and indentations to hold each individual bullet."

"Yeah, and?"

"It was obvious several bullets were missing."

"What?" I was stunned.

"Ali, we cannot jump to conclusions."

"I'm sorry, Matt. With the security precautions you mentioned, is there any doubt an angel, specifically an angel with super-secret access rights, stole those bullets and killed Felix?"

"Ali, I know how this looks on the surface, but what about motive, huh? Why would Gabriela, or any other high-ranking archangel, want him dead?"

"That's the million dollar question, isn't it?"

"We need to think about this before we act, Ali-gator. An archangel killing a vampire for no reason is cause for retaliation. It's cause for war."

I stopped pacing and glared at Matt.

"Ali, you know I'm right."

I looked away and tried to process everything I'd heard. I wanted to run to the Drakes and tell them all of this, but I feared they wouldn't be so level-headed in their response. Heck, after hearing this just now, I wanted to go after the angels and avenge Felix's death. But Matt was right. It wasn't enough simply knowing the bullets belonged to the Army. We needed to uncover who had done this and why. Suddenly I felt deflated in my mission. "This is bigger than me, Matt. I can't solve this mystery on my own."

"Ali, I don't know how much more I can help. I know I said I didn't think Gabriela knew I borrowed her access card, but she's been acting different lately, popping up when I least expect her as if she's trying to catch me in the act of doing something wrong."

"If she's not hiding a guilty conscience from having killed Felix, then she's probably on high alert since the two of us have been talking recently."

"Either way, I don't know how much more I can get away with."

"Oh please, Matt. What is she going to do to you, kick you out of the Army?"

"No," Matt responded defensively. "But there are punishments –"

"I'm so sick of hearing about these punishments. You know my society has punishments too. Fine, whatever. If you don't want to help, I guess I'll have to tell the Drakes what you told me and we'll solve Felix's murder."

"Ali, you can't do that."

"Why can't I? I just told you this is bigger than me–bullets made from the cross Jesus was crucified on, Vincent suspicious of my every move, Lucretia tailing me. I need help, Matt, and if you're not willing, I know the Drakes will be more than willing to hear this information and avenge their brother's death."

"Ali, use your head. If the Drakes hear this, they'll jump–"

"They'll jump to the only logical explanation."

Matt stared at me, mouth agape. "You can't."

"If you won't help me, then I have no choice but to find others who will." Matt ran a hand through his hair. "Help me prove an angel wasn't behind this. Help me prevent a war."

Matt's eyes locked on mine. "Fine."

I smiled. "Really?"

"Yes, really. I agree with you; something is going on. I don't know who's behind it or why. Gabriela isn't acting like herself. Not only is she stalking me, but she won't let Jenna leave the house by herself." Matt chuckled. "Little does Gabriela know Jenna sneaks out at night to be with Lorenzo."

"Excuse me?"

"Oh yeah, those two are like love-sick teenagers."

Good to know, I thought to myself. "I'll address Lorenzo later. But speaking of Jenna, what about Jenna's memories? Vincent altered them as a pawn in his scheme to sell his lies to me."

"They're still missing, but Gabriela and I did our best to fill in the gaps. Listen, Ali," Matt said, changing the subject. "We're not going to solve this now. I need to get back home before Gabriela becomes more suspicious than she already is. But I will help you. I'm trying to rationalize that my helping you is going to avoid a more immediate war than if you run back to the Drakes and tell them this. If that's the case, so be it. I'll handle whatever punishment the Army throws at me for working with the enemy. Maybe I'll recruit Jenna too. But please don't say anything to the Drakes until we figure this out."

"I promise," I said and made an X over my heart.

Matt nodded. "Okay." He approached me and awkwardly leaned in and gave me a hug, a far cry from the kiss I thought we were going to share earlier. "Okay, I'll be in touch." Matt pulled away and held me by my shoulders.

"Okay," I said.

I watched him walk to his truck and drive off, and only then did I exhale. His scent lingered in the air, triggering a growl from my stomach. I leaned against a tree and rubbed my neck where the bite wounds had been. I was famished; the two blood bags I'd had earlier had done little to satiate me. I retrieved my phone from my pocket and pulled up Max's hunting application. There was only one thing that could satisfy my craving and that was a long, stiff drink of human blood. And good news for me, there was a hunting spot only a vampire hop, skip and a jump away.

Chapter 10

Deja vu struck as I drove the Corvette on the winding driveway leading to Castle Adena. Marlo had texted and said I needed to get there ASAP. She didn't indicate what the rush was about, but given the situation the last time I had ignored her calls and texts, I thought it best to respond and obey this time. Plus, I had ulterior motives for wanting to return to the castle. There was a certain painting I wanted to revisit.

I parked the car and scrambled out of it and to the front door. Before I could knock, Vincent pulled open the door. He blocked the entryway with his body as he scanned me from head to toe. "Well hello to you too," I said, my hand still balled and in knocking position.

He scoffed. "I see you've fed."

I dropped my arm and cocked my head. "Why thank you, Captain State the Obvious. Yes, I've fed."

"What have you been feeding on?" Vincent demanded.

"What is this?" I questioned as I pushed past him.

"Are you killing humans again?"

"Um, hello–I'm a vampire. I have to kill the occasional human in order to survive."

"Stop making light of this. You know what I mean. Are you binging again?"

I huffed. "You have a lot of nerve, Vincent. You know damn well that Max helped me get back on the wagon; after all, you tricked me into returning to the castle where I was forced into rehab. And I haven't fallen off of the wagon since. And by the way, I'm allowed to hunt humans."

"Yes, but–"

"Leave her alone, brother," Max said as he entered the great room.

"Thank you, Max," I said as I greeted him and we kissed each other's cheeks. I felt vindicated having someone in my corner.

"I can tell Allison accessed the hunting application. She's hunting according to plan."

I smirked and crinkled my nose like a child, telling Vincent without saying a word, *I told you so*.

"Besides," Max continued before Vincent could interject. "Once she accessed the app, I had her followed, you know, just in case. That vampire verified Allison stuck to the plan."

"You did what?" I questioned and jumped back a step. "You spied on me?"

"Can you blame them?" Marlo asked as she entered the room.

"So there's seriously no trust here?" I looked around the room at the three Drake siblings who all returned hardened expressions. "Is this why you demanded I come back here? To accuse me of doing something I shouldn't be doing?"

"No, that's not the reason," Marlo responded.

"Good, because I thought this might have something to do with Felix. Have you discovered anything new, any clues about who killed him?"

The three exchanged glances like they knew something. "No, we haven't," Vincent said. "Have you?"

My eye twitched. If the Drakes had me followed to ensure I stuck to my diet, did they also have me followed when I wasn't hunting? Could they have possibly known I had met up with Matt at my parents' crypt? If there was a spy, could he or she have heard what Matt and I talked about? *And trust no one. Not even my siblings.* Felix's warning crossed my mind. "No," I said. "In fact, I don't even know where to begin looking. I thought that's why you called me here today, to devise a plan." Silence. "So that's not why we're here today?" More silence. I didn't know what was going on. Why were the Drakes being so evasive? "Has anybody gone back to the scene of the crime to find any clues? What about the police?"

"The police?" Vincent scoffed. "What a human-like thing to say. We can't involve the police. That's too dangerous, we could expose our existence."

"Okay, then what? Why are we here?"

"We need to wait for Lorenzo," Marlo said. She was all business-like, not the usual motherly Marlo I knew and much preferred.

I looked around the room and noticed the patriarch was absent. "Where is Lorenzo?"

As if on cue, Lorenzo walked through the front door.

"Well, well, well, look what the cat dragged in," I said and then whistled. Lorenzo's ratty hair was pulled back into a messy ponytail. His shirt and pants were wrinkled as if he'd spent the night in them. "Booty call with my best friend?"

"As a matter of fact," Lorenzo cleared his throat, "I did spend the night with Jenna."

The muscles in my jaw tightened. The way he had stated that so calmly, like it was no big deal, got under my skin. My cheeks warmed. "I don't want you hanging around Jenna."

Lorenzo scoffed. "You can't tell me what to do."

"Oh, really? What kind of hypocrisy is this? I can't hang out with Matt, but you can hang out with Jenna? Have you forgotten that

Gabriela declared Jenna a member of the flock, essentially making Jenna one of them?"

"That's a big technicality," Lorenzo challenged. "Gabriela can declare whatever she wants, but the only way to become an angel or an archangel is to be born one. So there's no risk of *our* relationship sparking a war."

I ground my teeth. The inequity of the situation burned me. How was it Matt and I were allowed to marry when we didn't know I was a vampire in waiting and Matt an archangel, but the moment we knew what each other were, boom, we couldn't be together for fear of sparking a war between age old enemies. The marriage was permitted when it was convenient for Saint Michael's Army to essentially have an undercover angel living with a descendant. But once their benefit was eliminated, our marriage was dissolved. The truth had destroyed my marriage, but I'd be damned if I were going to let it ruin my future.

"That's all fine and dandy, but do you think Gabriela will take kindly to a vampire dating someone who lives under her roof?"

"She'll never find out as long as you don't say anything."

"You're not as stealthy as you think, Lorenzo. Matt is on to you. He knows you and Jenna are sneaking around. Don't you think it's only a matter of time before Gabriela finds out?"

"I don't care what Gabriela has to say."

"Matthew?" Marlo shrieked. "How do you know Matthew knows anything about Lorenzo and Jenna?"

Busted, I thought. Why had I opened my big mouth and all but confess to the Drakes I'd been seeing Matt?

"Allison," Max admonished. I looked at Vincent. His cheeks flexed and eyes clouded over. "Have you been seeing Matthew?" he asked through gritted teeth.

"Now that's cause for a war, Allison," Lorenzo chided.

I opened my mouth but was cut off by Marlo.

"It is, but that's not the reason we're all here today."

"Yes, sister," Lorenzo said. "What was so urgent we all had to gather at a moment's notice?"

"A courier bird delivered this earlier today." Marlo held up a scroll.

"Courier bird?" I questioned.

"Yes, a raven," Marlo responded.

I shook my head, not understanding.

Lorenzo walked past me. "The Ruling Council uses ravens to deliver messages."

"The Ruling Council?" I mumbled. "Now what do they want?"

"Answers," Marlo responded as Lorenzo grabbed the scroll and unrolled it.

"Answers about what?" I questioned. "Didn't we address all of their questions back in March?"

"Actually, they're looking for answers about something you're quite familiar with," Lorenzo said.

I plucked the note from Lorenzo's hand and groaned as I read the message. "Sam and Brian's murders." I dropped the letter and began pacing. "Those killings happened months ago. Why can't the Council let it go already?"

"Because the murders are unsolved and still in the news," Max responded.

"Yeah, thanks to Sam's father and the way the media fawns over him," I said.

"Had you been more discriminating in your hunts, my dear," Vincent said, "you wouldn't be in this pickle."

I stopped in my tracks and glared at Vincent. "Seriously?"

Vincent smirked.

"Allison," Max said. "You know the Council is on edge about these two cases and will continue to be until they're solved or until the media stops covering them."

"Well let's hope for the latter because if the cases are solved, I'm no longer going to exist."

"How long until a crime is considered a cold case?" Marlo asked as she put a hand on my shoulder. I appreciated the kind thought and smiled at her. I grabbed the letter from her hand.

"I would guess once clues and tips stop being reported to the police, but considering there are no new clues, it's the incessant media coverage keeping this front of mind for all of Northeast Ohio that's the problem." I reread the letter. "And the formality of it all. The Council requests my presence," I mockingly imitated. "As if I have a choice!"

"Unfortunately there's no choice involved when the Council fears one of their rules may have been broken."

"Did you know anything about this?" I asked Lorenzo as I pointed at the letter.

"No, Allison, I didn't. Had I known, I would have given you advance warning."

"How can they exclude one of the seated Council members from decisions such as this?"

"They can very easily if they suspect that the Council member would side with the person with whom they want to speak."

"And Lorenzo has vigorously defended you to the seated members since March," Max added. "Of course they're going to assume Lorenzo would side with you."

"I mean, I get it, but if they want to talk to me, all they have to do is call. I haven't fled…." I stopped when I realized what I was about to say. But I had fled. I had run off with Vincent to explore places I had only dreamed of while leaving behind the media circus of Sam and Brian's deaths—a media circus that could expose the existence of vampires and lead to my demise for having revealed that secret. The Council was rightfully mad at me. And I was rightfully mad at Vincent for aiding in my current predicament. Had I never fled in the first place, this situation wouldn't be as tenuous. "Never mind, I get it. But can I change first?" I was still wearing the clothes from the day before when Matt and I met at the cemetery, the same clothes I had recently hunted in which were coated with the scent of my latest victim. I didn't need the Council smelling the evidence, even it if was a sanctioned kill.

"Of course," Marlo said. "I think that's for the best. You still have clothes in your room upstairs. Here, let me take you."

"No," I snipped. I took a breath and regained my composure. "Ah, thanks, Marlo, but that's not necessary. I can find my way."

I took the steps four at a time until arriving at the hallway. I scurried down the corridor, opened the door and slipped into the room. I opened the armoire and grabbed the first outfit, quickly changing out of my dirty clothes and into the new ensemble. A change of clothes was the last thing on my mind. I was looking forward to another visit with Felix's magical painting.

I zipped and buttoned my jeans and wiggled into a shirt. Zipping up my boots, I took a quick look in the mirror, fluffed my hair and then ran over to the painting. I cracked my back and closed my eyes, taking in deep breaths to calm my racing heart. A few inhales later and I allowed my hunting instincts to takeover. When I opened my eyes, I expected to see colored speckles skating over the canvas, like I had seen last time, but that wasn't the case. Instead, I saw each brushstroke that made up the larger painting. There wasn't a single speck out of place waiting to form a secret message.

"What the heck," I muttered. I extended my hands to the canvas and rubbed my fingers across the surface trying to shake the magic into motion. I reigned in my senses and silently cursed at the painting. I wanted another clue. I needed another clue. "Why are you doing this to me?"

And then something caught my eye. A sliver of paper stuck out from behind the lower corner of the painting. I bent over for closer inspection. It appeared to be an envelope wedged between the wall and painting. "What's this?" I whispered. I glanced at the painting and did a double take. Specks of color darted over the canvas, the black pixels already forming a pulsating blob. The black paint contracted and expanded and formed a point. The two lines that made the point moved away from each other forming a V, before sharply turning and heading toward each other. Before touching, the lines turned again and moved away ever so slightly, fanning out. Once the movement stopped, the remaining black particles backfilled the outline of an arrow. The shape moved in a wave-like motion, appearing like a cinema marquee, pointing toward the corner where I'd already discovered the envelope.

"Better late than never," I joked and winked at the painting.

I snatched the paper from behind the painting and saw it was addressed to me. This didn't surprise me given the plethora of messages I'd recently received. I removed the paper, unfolded it and found a large black X in the middle of it. Under that, it read, "X marks the spot."

I looked at the painting hoping the paint would have rearranged itself into something more descriptive, preferably a direct answer, but instead the painting had returned to its original state.

"Awesome. Another ambiguous clue."

A knock on the door interrupted my thoughts. As I approached and grabbed the doorknob, the person on the other side was already twisting it.

"Allison," the butler said. "Are you ready to meet with the Ruling Council?"

The man who greeted me was the same person who had escorted me to this room the day I had found out about Felix's murder. But unlike that day, today he wore his hair loose. It fell past his shoulders in flowing, brown waves. Light glinted off his natural highlights, and a memory was triggered. This was the same vampire I had followed out of the chapel at the funeral; the same vampire who had lead me to the statue I'd been dreaming about and ultimately, in combination with the written clue he had given me, led me to my parents' crypt and the discovery of another clue. His eyes moved toward my hand with the note and he smiled, as if satisfied I had found it.

"Who are you?" I demanded.

The butler pressed his index finger to my lips to hush me, while pointing downstairs, indicating the vampires below could hear us.

"Did you leave this for me?" I whispered, shaking the note in his direction. "How did you know about the code word my parents used when I was a child?"

He waved his finger to hush me; vampire ears could pick up a whisper if those downstairs were, for some reason, listening for me. He shook his head indicating he had not planted the note for me.

"Then who did?" I mouthed.

The man raised an eyebrow.

"Felix?"

He grinned and grabbed the envelope from my hand. Reaching into his coat pocket, he retrieved a pen, scribbled something on the paper and handed it back to me.

I looked twice to ensure my eyes weren't deceiving me. I looked up, intending to berate the butler with a barrage of questions, but he was gone, his signature mist left behind where he had stood. I looked back at the note: *the truth will set you free.*

Chapter 11

I tucked the note in my pants pocket and headed downstairs. Back in the great room, only Marlo and Max were there. Marlo bit her nails as she paced the length of the wall and Max lay on a chaise with his eyes closed. He sat up when he heard me enter the room.

"What's the name of the butler I keep seeing around here?" I asked as I pointed over my shoulder in the direction of the second floor.

Marlo stopped chewing her nails. "What butler?"

"Long brown hair, brown eyes, about this tall." I held my hand above my head. "He was here the day I found out about Felix's death too."

"I don't know who you're talking about, Ali," Max said as he stood. He grabbed my hands. "We haven't brought any of the staff back since finding out about our brother. But—"

"Well, well, well," a familiar voice bellowed. "Look who it is."

I turned toward the doorway leading to the dining room. Titus marched out like he owned the place, with Lorenzo on his heels, followed by Marguerite and Amil.

"I thought we were going to Rattlesnake Island," I whispered to Marlo who had scrambled to my side.

"I never said we were going there," she whispered back.

"But the letter—"

"It only requested your presence. They knew we'd call you and you'd show up here. Their plan must have been to come here before we departed for the island."

"It's the reckless one," Marguerite quipped in response to Titus' comment.

The motley crew heading toward me looked angry, their heavy footsteps echoing off the walls, their stern facial expressions as cold as ice. I thought I'd lighten the mood. "Missing a member, aren't you?" I asked.

Titus scoffed, stopping within three feet of me. His ghastly eyes took my breath away, his irises so pale his eyes practically blended with his skin tone. "You think you can still ask the questions? Tsk, tsk, tsk, haven't you learned anything from our previous encounters? You don't get to ask the questions, Allison. I ask the questions."

I bit my tongue to prevent myself from saying something I was certain I'd regret. My aggravation with the Council's unease, my dislike of Jenna's newfound taste in men, my situation with Matt, and all of these senseless clues were feeding my growing frustration. But I somehow needed to let the frustrations go for the moment.

"It is a valid question," Lorenzo said. He broke from the pack and stood in between them and us. "And a question I also have. We can't have an official Council meeting without having all of the seated members present, like the meetings I'm sure you had before delivering your message via courier."

Lorenzo glared at Titus who cleared his throat. "Are you accusing the Council of convening without all members present?"

"The circumstance lends itself to that. Mere hours ago we receive notice that you demand Allison's presence. Why would you demand her presence if the three or four of you hadn't been discussing matters?"

"So you have it all figured out then, don't you?"

"Look Titus, I'm not accusing you or the other Council members of anything. But things appear a bit suspect, so why don't you start talking?"

"I don't like your tone, Lorenzo. I'm the chief seated member of the Ruling Council. Show some respect."

Titus stepped forward, going toe-to-toe with Lorenzo. They were the same height, but Lorenzo had more muscle. It appeared that physically, Lorenzo could take Titus in battle, but physical stature didn't matter much when you were dealing with vampires who were thousands of years old and outfitted with equal supernatural strength. Marguerite grabbed Titus' arm.

"There's no need for this macho showmanship," Marguerite said. Titus retreated, his eyes still trained on Lorenzo. "Lucretia isn't here because she doesn't need to be. This isn't a formal Ruling Council meeting."

"That's right," Titus chimed in. "Lucretia is off researching something, God only knows what. She promised her time away is well spent, and what she's looking into is big. She'll inform us once she has all of the details."I shuddered at the thought of Lucretia and her research. She was researching me and Lord help the Drakes and me if she uncovered the truth about my lineage. The Drakes had kept the truth about descendants from the Council and every other vampire out there. Who knew how the vampire community would react once they discovered the truth, especially Titus, given how much he relished his role as lead seated member and the power it afforded him.

"And her presence isn't needed here today. We requested this impromptu meeting after seeing yet another TV broadcast about two particular unsolved murder cases."

Titus and the two Council members behind him focused their eyes on me like a laser to a target.

"I don't know what more you want me to say," I blurted.

"We've had to change our hunting patterns due to the media attention," Amil huffed liked a child whose toy had been taken away.

"I'm certainly sorry about your inconvenience, but I'm sure this will blow over soon."

"Oh really?" Marguerite hissed. "You said that months ago, but here we still are—the cases aren't closed and the media is all over this as much as they were when the bodies were first discovered."

"If Sam's uncle would stop strong-arming the media into continuous coverage, this would all blow over and be done with."

"But that isn't happening," Titus said. "Councilman Thornberg was a prominent member of the community long before being elected to office. He has enough money to throw at this situation until it's solved. And that, my dear, does not bode well for you."

"They're not going to find anything. I swear."

"Your words mean little. All of the proof Felix had given us about your mortal kills while you were parading around North America panned out, but Felix neglected any mention of these crimes."

I sucked in a long draw of air. "That wasn't Felix's fault. He didn't—the Drakes didn't—know about those kills since they were so recent. Once back in Ohio, I wasn't myself. I was distracted and reckless. But your threats at the March Council meeting registered with me. As soon as I realized I hadn't covered my tracks with those murders, I went back to the scenes and cleaned them up. No evidence was left behind. The bite marks were concealed. There's no way the police are going to expect vampirism, especially as such a thing doesn't exist for humans outside of movies and books."

"Still, that's of little comfort to us," Marguerite said. "We have two communities who have been on edge for months. Everyone and everything is being viewed under a microscope. Where we once roamed freely without a second thought, we're now looking over our shoulders."

"Don't you think you're being a tad bit paranoid? Do you think humans are logically going to conclude vampires killed Sam and Brian?"

"There you go again asking questions," Titus hissed. "It doesn't matter if we're paranoid or not. The fact is, things have changed for us, and we don't like change. You need to fix this." Titus sounded like a playground bully trying to get his way in an impossible situation.

"How? Oh, I'm sorry, that was another question."

Titus glowered at me while Amil answered the question. "Take care of the current problem."

"Wait a minute. You want me to fix this by killing Councilman Thornberg? Because his death wouldn't draw any suspicions, right?"

"Then make it look like an accident," Marguerite demanded.

I went to respond, but Marlo stopped me. "How about we give it a little more time, huh?" Titus protested but Marlo raised her hand. "Sam and Brian were killed in March; it's now September and the police are no closer to solving the cases now than they were then. Let the Councilman throw his money at the problem, but the reality is as soon as the next big story comes up, these murders will be long forgotten by the media who will be chomping at the bit for a fresh story."

"There's no guarantee of that," Titus said.

"No, there isn't. But other than the Councilman's bloviating, there's nothing new with the cases to cover. The reporters are running out of angles to present. Once the next sensational murder happens, or some natural disaster, or some celebrity does something stupid, Sam and Brian will be long forgotten, their cases reclassified as cold."

"I can tell you're not happy with that approach," Max said. "But honestly, what else can be done at this point? Humans still think our kind is something that exists only in the movies. Allison's actions haven't revealed our existence; therefore, you can't punish her. There's nothing to punish her for. And killing her doesn't resolve the media issue."

"Fine," Titus resigned. "But this needs to go away, and go away soon." He paced, and the rest of us watched, waiting for his next reaction. "And speaking of crimes, have you discovered anything about who may have killed your brother?"

"That's a family matter," Lorenzo hissed, "and none of your business."

Titus smirked. "Ah, but it is our business. You see, Lorenzo, nothing, and I mean nothing, has been the same around here since this one arrived." Titus stuck a pointy fingernail in my direction. "Tell me, Allison. What do you know about Felix's murder?"

"Me? Why would you think I know anything about Felix's killer?"

Titus cocked his head, eyes narrowing, lips pulled tight into a joker's grin.

"Oh come on. You can't be serious. I certainly did not kill Felix!"

"This is preposterous," Lorenzo yelled. "You may be seated members of the Ruling Council, and you," Lorenzo poked Titus on the chest, "may be the chief Council member, but that doesn't give any of you the right to show up on our doorstep and sling these sorts of allegations."

"Oh, I see I've touched a nerve," Titus cooed. "Have you forgotten? As the chief Ruling Council member, I can do whatever I want, Lorenzo." The two stood nose-to-nose, locked in a stare down. Tension crackled in the air. I was afraid to move, fearing the slightest movement would set off a fight like a spark around dynamite. I shifted my eyes from one Council member to the next and all I saw were icy stares. I felt the need to say something to cut the tension.

"Something is amiss," I whispered.

"What was that?" Titus demanded, not breaking his staring competition with Lorenzo.

"We are investigating Felix's murder, but we don't know yet who killed him or why."

"How was he killed?" Titus asked as he stepped around Lorenzo.

Now was one of those moments where I wished I could think fast and come up with a response that was something other than the truth. I surely couldn't tell the Council that Felix was murdered with a wooden bullet. The Drakes and I wanted to keep that information to ourselves until we understood what it meant. And I certainly couldn't tell everyone the bullets were crafted from the cross Jesus was crucified on. I wanted to keep that information to myself until I knew who used the bullets to kill Felix.

"Come now," Titus shouted. "What is it? It was evident at the funeral that he wasn't killed in the traditional manner as he looked remarkably well."

"He was shot," Max responded.

"Max!" I exclaimed. He shrugged his shoulders.

"A wooden bullet, to be exact," Marlo added.

I whirled around and looked at Marlo, but she refused to make eye contact.

"But not just any wooden bullet," Lorenzo continued. "A wooden bullet that sears the flesh of a vampire."

Titus, Marguerite and Amil simultaneously gasped at the revelation.

"Hexed bullets," Marguerite murmured. "This can only mean one thing."

"I agree," Amil said, as if reading Marguerite's mind.

"Gypsies," Titus cursed.

"Gypsies?" I shrieked. "What?"

"Of course," Amil said. "It's the only logical explanation."

121

"Who else has magical capabilities to create a weapon to kill vampires?" Marguerite asked to no one in particular.

"It makes sense," Lorenzo said.

I looked around the room and couldn't believe what was happening. The Council had made a snap decision that gypsies were behind Felix's murder without being presented with any tangible evidence to back up the claim. They were hungry for vengeance, probably since they couldn't punish me for my crimes. I supposed I should be thankful their anger was placed elsewhere, but I couldn't get past the knot in my stomach telling me that if I didn't intervene, innocent blood would be on my hands without having killed a single person. Yes, I wanted Felix's murderer caught and punished, but I wanted to ensure we had the right person.

"You can't be so sure," I interjected.

"Why not?" Titus hissed and slithered over to me. "Do you have another explanation?"

"Well no, not yet, but you can't assume gypsies did this without having any concrete proof to back your claims."

"Concrete proof?" Titus asked. He forced me back until I was pinned against a wall, his breath hot on my face. "How about a little history lesson, dear? I know you're a young vampire, but I surely would have thought your coven would have given you this history lesson. Oh yes, that's right, you were off parading around the world like an irresponsible, spoiled brat. So let me catch you up." Spittle spattered my face, causing me to jerk, but I didn't dare raise a hand to wipe it away, fearing Titus would mistake that for a defensive move. "Vampires and gypsies are centuries old enemies. We've disliked each other from day one. Sure, many truces have been reached between the two societies over the years, but they've never lasted. It's always a given that a new elder wants to flex his muscle and does something stupid to remind vampires how dangerous gypsies are to our existence. They've proven that time and again. This, Allison, is their latest scheme to remind us that they can use their magic to inflict pain on us. But we won't stand for it, will we?" Titus turned as he shouted that to the room.

"No," everyone, the Drakes included, responded.

"This act of war against our society calls for a response," Titus yelled. "We must act swiftly and with force."

"We must send a message that we are not weak and will not be intimidated," Marguerite said.

"I agree," Lorenzo added. "We must convene a Council session promptly to discuss our response."

"Response to what?" I asked. Silence fell over the room and all attention turned to me like stage lights to an actress. "A response to your suspicions?"

"Do you not want justice for your fallen coven member?" Amil questioned.

"I do, but I want proof that points to the true culprit. We can't act on suspicions. Listen to yourselves. You want a fight, and a fight is what you're going to get if you attack the gypsies. My coven, by the way, gave me this history lesson, Titus. So I know about the origins of the vampire/gypsy rift. You don't want to get tangled in another battle with them and risk losing hundreds of vampires all for what? Acting on unfounded suspicions?"

"Hmm," Titus purred. "You're so quick to defend the gypsies. That must mean you have another theory. If not the gypsies, then who else would be behind this?"

"Well, I don't know," I lied, not wanting to reveal any of the information Matt had shared with me. "But we need to take our time and fully investigate this to ensure we punish the appropriate person or persons and not send legions of vampires to their deaths in the process."

"There's still so much that is human about you," Titus said.

"What does that mean?"

"Your mortal justice system in this country calls for innocence before proven guilty. You must show beyond a reasonable doubt that someone is guilty before you sentence him or her. But that type of mentality in the vampire realm will get you killed." Titus leered into my face, pausing momentarily, before backing away.

"He's right, Allison," Vincent said, almost pleading.

"So you'd rather attack gypsies based on your past history rather than take a few days and try to figure this out?"

"Yes. This isn't our first run in with the gypsies. This has their fingerprints all over it. So unless you have another theory, this means war."

What I had wanted to say was on the tip of my tongue, but I couldn't let the words pass for fear of the retribution it would mean for the angels.

"Well then," Titus said, "now that that is settled, we'll convene tonight on Rattlesnake Island with all members of the Ruling Council and determine how to proceed."

The Drakes concurred, parting pleasantries were exchanged and Titus and his crew headed for the door.

"Have you considered the possibility that angels were behind this?" I asked. I couldn't let the Council act against a faction we didn't even know had committed the crime. I hated to serve up the angels; I didn't want to see harm come to Matt, but I had to say something to give this group pause.

The departing Council members stopped in their tracks. The Drakes froze like statues. After a few moments of silence, Lorenzo asked what I was talking about.

"Gypsies aren't our only enemies," I responded.

"Why would the angels have done this?" Marlo asked.

"Why would the gypsies?" I countered.

"Do you have proof angels are behind this?" Lorenzo demanded.

I took a moment to gather my thoughts. I didn't want to divulge all of the information Matt had given me. The Drakes and the Council didn't need to know at this point that the bullets that had killed Felix were part of collection of crafted ammunition privy to select members of the archangel ranks. That fact would more than likely be what this crowd needed to declare war, and I didn't want that. I couldn't do that. I merely wanted to divert attention away from the gypsies while offering another plausible alternative in the hopes of gaining more time to investigate and to postpone an unnecessary war.

"Well?" Titus asked.

"We know there's an army of angels here on earth, sanctioned by the Lord, whose mission is to protect mortal souls from being damned by our bite, right?"

"Of course," Amil said.

"Well, isn't that enough motive for all of you? I mean you were willing to jump on the gypsy bandwagon based on your past history, so why shouldn't the angels also be part of our persons of interest list based on our history with them?"

"Allison has a point," Marlo murmured.

Whispers broke out among the ranks.

"Does this have anything to do with you hanging out with Matthew?" Vincent spat Matt's name with disgust.

I was taken off guard by the question.

"Who is Matthew?" Titus asked. "Is this the same Matthew I heard about at Caverns Point Park?"

"Suffice it to say he's an ex-husband," I responded. "Well technically, he's a widower."

"You left your husband to become a vampire?" Titus questioned. "You grow more intriguing by the moment."

"Answer my question, Allison," Vincent demanded. Red tinted the whites of his eyes.

"Yes, Vincent. This is the reason I've been hanging around Matt. I suspected angels could be behind Felix's murder, but unlike all of you, I was searching for proof. So I've been hanging out with Matt in hopes of unearthing some clues."

"Your former husband is an angel?" Marguerite asked.

"Archangel, to be precise."

"You're an interesting woman, Allison Carmichael," Marguerite responded. "Once this is all behind us, and if you survive, I think we all need to take the time to get to know you a little better."

Great, just what I wanted–more unwanted Ruling Council attention. Just who I wanted to hang out with once I was in the clear from Sam and Brian's murders.

"Allison, why didn't you tell us?" Marlo asked. "We could have helped you with this investigation."

"I didn't tell any of you since it's against vampire law to hang out with angels. I knew if I'd have told you what I wanted to do, you'd be against it, so I took matters into my own hands."

"It is brilliant," Max said.

"What is?" Vincent hissed.

"Matt is Allison's former husband and an archangel. You were married for what, seven years?"

"Yes," I responded.

"Feelings from a relationship of that duration don't go away overnight. So Allison used her relationship with Matt to get close to him in order to investigate our brother's death. It's brilliant." I gulped at Max's summary of the situation, and although a lie, it was a good one and would keep me out of hot water with everyone else for having been hanging around with Matt—well everyone except Vincent.

"But that doesn't—"

I cut off Vincent, fearing he'd reveal that I'd been spotted with Matt before Felix's death and blow Max's theory right out of the water. "That's right, Max. That's exactly what I was doing."

"Thank you, Allison, for risking your life to solve Felix's murder," Max said.

Guilt settled in with that remark. Max was giving me more credit than I deserved. Sure, I wanted to solve Felix's murder, but only because I had a strong inclination something more sinister was going on that no one was talking about. I didn't know who knew what, but I was going to find out.

"Maybe I've misjudged you," Titus said as he straightened his jacket. "It appears you've been sacrificing more to solve Felix's murder than his own siblings. You have the full support of the Council and any resources you may need to continue this investigation, Allison."

I couldn't believe the turn of events. Now if I could only get the Council off my back for Sam and Brian's murders.

"You're giving her the green light to work with angels?" Vincent questioned.

I walked to his side and put an arm over his shoulder. "Come now, dear, it's all in an effort to capture Felix's killer. You can't be mad about that, can you?"

"Yes, I am giving her the green light," Titus responded. "But once the investigation is over, no more fraternizing with the enemy. Got it?"

I nodded with no intent of letting the Ruling Council, or anyone else, dictate who I could or couldn't associate with.

"And Allison, work fast. We want justice sooner rather than later."

My phone vibrated, and I retrieved it from my pocket. I accidentally removed the note as well. It fell to the floor. I scooped it up and caught Vincent's searing glare. I quickly glanced at my phone. It was a text from Matt indicating he had found something and wanted to share with me immediately. "You bet. In fact, my next clue has arrived." I held up the phone and waved it in the air.

"Do you need help, Allison?" Marlo offered.

"Thanks, but I got this. Don't want to tip off Matt that something is wrong."

I thanked the Council for their support in the matter and then turned. "I'll see you later," I said to the Drakes; well at least to the three of them who were still in the room. Vincent was gone.

Chapter 12

"Heads up," I yelled as I walked into my house. I tossed a prepaid cellphone in Matt's direction.

He caught the device. "What's this?"

"A new phone. If the Drakes are monitoring me through my phone, then chances are Gabriela is monitoring you through yours. My new number is already programmed in it."

"What do you mean the Drakes are monitoring you through your phone?"

"I, um, had an errand to run after meeting you at the cemetery. They saw that I accessed an app on my phone and had a vampire tail me to ensure I wasn't doing something I shouldn't have been."

"Oh, wow." Matt flipped open the phone and smiled. "Cute," he said, turning the phone toward me. I had taken a snapshot of myself and used it as the picture that would appear on screen when he dialed my number.

"Thanks. So what did you find?"

"Actually it's what Jenna and I may have found.""Jenna?"

"Yeah, Ali, I started thinking about things—our recent conversations, the fact Vincent is a historian, all of the books he placed at your house, Lucretia tailing you and so on. I needed to talk things through with someone and I certainly couldn't talk to Gabriela. So I pulled Jenna into this."

"Matt, I understand you need to talk to someone, but Jenna? She's already been through so much having her memories altered by Vincent, kidnapped by Lucious' groupies and then everything she witnessed on Rattlesnake Island. Do you think she's up to this?"

"Your best friend is a tough cookie. Besides," Matt chuckled, "Jenna is dating a vampire, for God's sake. I think she can handle a little research."

"Ugh. Dating? Is it that serious?"

"Well, dating as much as she can given she has to sneak behind Gabriela's back, but it appears Jenna has figured it out. And who knows how much Lorenzo has told her about the vampire world. So yes, I think Jenna is more than capable of getting involved with this."

"I don't want to see anything happen to her, Matt. She's a mortal with knowledge of vampire existence and wasn't born an angel so she doesn't have the full protection of the Army. If something happened to her, I couldn't forgive myself."

"I wouldn't let anything happen to her, Ali."

"Yeah, I know Matt, but what about when she's out with Lorenzo?"

"Do you think he'd allow something bad to come of her? He knows she's your best friend."

I contemplated that for a moment. "No, I guess not. So what did you and Jenna find?"

"I was hoping she would fill you in, but she isn't–" The doorbell chimed. "Speak of the Devil."

"Jenna's here?"

I rushed to the door and pulled it open. "Jenna, how are you?" I gave her a big hug and she reciprocated. Pulling away, I said, "Thank you for helping Matt and me with all of this."

"No worries, you know I'd help you with anything." She walked past me and I shut the door. "What are best friends for?"

"You still consider us best friends?"

"Of course. Why wouldn't I?"

"The whole turning into a vampire thing doesn't get in the way of our friendship?"

"Pfft? That?" Jenna mockingly waved her hand. "Of course not."

If Jenna could look past the fact I was a vampire, then why couldn't Matt? Was it the fact he was born an archangel? My face flushed as I thought about how unfair life could be.

"You were able to sneak out without Gabriela noticing?" Matt asked.

"I think so. I wove through the back roads before getting on the freeway. I didn't see anyone following me.""Good," Matt said.

"What's this I hear about you dating a vampire?" I asked.

"Oh no you don't, Ali. You get no say in who I date."

"But he's a vampire, Jenna. You're in danger simply by hanging around him."

"You're a vampire too, and I'm hanging around you now."

"Yeah, and I almost attacked you the night of the Halloween party. Jenna, I could have killed you."

"I'm not concerned. Lorenzo told me you went through Max's vampire detox and have your urge for human blood under control. I trust I'll be perfectly safe in your presence." She smiled. It struck me how she spoke of Lorenzo and Max as if she had been life-long friends with them. And then I realized if Lorenzo had told Jenna about my sobriety, maybe she had relayed the information to Matt and was one of the reasons he had been agreeable to meeting up with me this past July. "So do you want to hear what we found or what?"

"Yes, of course."

We gathered around the coffee table. I sat on the floor while Matt and Jenna sat on opposite ends of the couch.

"We found something in your family tree."

"What?"

"Yeah. Matt mentioned one of the clues you found referenced your family tree."

"It took a little research," Matt said, "but we were able to piece together your family tree using public records and ancestry records we obtained online."

"And?" I twirled my hand to speed the update along.

"We started on your mother's side," Jenna said.

I narrowed my eyes."Matt filled me in on some details. He wanted to start there since the Devil's venom had been passed down to you through her side of the family."

"What else do you know about me?"

"We'll save that for another time." She smiled.

"So what did you find?"

"Well, it was difficult at first. We examined your family tree and compared it to files the Army has maintained on all of the descendants and vampire covens."

"What? The Army has records on us?"

"Of course we do, Ali." Matt responded. "It's our job to protect mortals and in order to do that we need to know who the enemy, I mean, who all of the vampires, are."

"I see. And what did you find?"

"I didn't find anything," Jenna said.

"But I noticed something," Matt continued. "Actually I noticed two things. First, there appears to be either a gap in your tree or I'm missing some information."

"What do you mean?"

"As I traced back through your ancestors, I noticed what I would equate to a blip. Meaning your ancestry records showed one descendant, but Army records have a different name. I'm not sure if it's anything to be concerned about since many of these records were kept manually way back when, and I'm talking really far back, over 1,000 years ago. I didn't see any other anomalies like that, but this is still on my radar."

"Interesting. What else did you find?"

"Something else caught my attention. There was a familiarity with a string of surnames I came across. Those names matched in both sets of records but I can't put a finger on why those names struck a chord with me. And oddly enough, the familiarity abruptly ended with the blip I found."

"What do you mean by familiarity? You've seen the names before?"

"The names were familiar to me. When I read them, I felt like I'd seen the names before but couldn't place them."

"What are some of the names?"

"Miell, Michalik, Mielnik, Mikkelsen. There are more too."

"Did you look into it further? Did you discover why the names were familiar to you?"

"I tried but was interrupted by Gabriela. We wanted to share this news with you to see if any of it made sense."

"None of it makes sense to me, Matt. I mean, I've never dug through my family history because I've never had a need to. How would I know what any of this means?"

"Have you found any other clues that may help?"

I scoffed. "Yeah, I found another clue, but I'm not sure it'll help with this."

"What's the clue?" Jenna asked. She scooted to the edge of the couch.

I reached into my pocket and tossed the folded paper onto the coffee table. Matt grabbed it and unfolded it as Jenna moved closer to get a look.

"X marks the spot, huh?" Jenna said.

"Right? I mean what in the world does that mean?"

"Where did you find this?" Matt asked.

"Behind the corner of a painting in what was formerly my room at Castle Adena."

"Are you sure the clue wasn't planted by someone in the castle wanting to throw you off?"

I mulled the question for a moment. "I'm pretty sure it was left for me by Felix or someone working with Felix." Visions of the paint pixels forming an arrow pulsating in the direction of the note made me certain of that.

"What does it all mean?" Jenna asked to no one in particular. "One clue is in your family tree, then there was the Ulee reference to the code word you and your parents used when you were a kid, and now X marks the spot?"

"I haven't the slightest idea." I flung myself onto the couch next to Matt and covered my eyes with my hand.

"Hey, we'll figure it out." He squeezed my leg. I separated the fingers covering my eyes and looked at Matt. His warm smile greeted me. I dropped my hand and shifted my head on the cushion to get a better view of his handsome face. Butterflies danced in my stomach and a wave of tingles emanated from my core. God, I missed Matt. Was there any way we could ever be together?

"Yeah, we'll figure *this* out," I replied.

Jenna cleared her throat, reminding me she was still in the room. I rolled my head back and stared at the ceiling. The sound of screeching tires disrupted the momentary silence.

"Who could that be?" Matt asked as he jumped off the couch. Before Jenna or I could react, the front door swung open and Gabriela stomped into the living room. She rambled in Spanish, arms flailing, stacks of multicolor bangles clanking, while incessantly tapping her stilettos. My stomach lurched at the realization we'd been busted again, and this time with Jenna. She let out an "ay dios mio" and then a long breath as her glare calculatingly moved between the three of us.

"Gabriela–" Matt started.

"Aye, aye, aye," she yelled and held up a hand. "I don't want to hear it."

I pushed myself off the couch and said, "You can't barge into my home like this."

"And vampires can't socialize with archangels, but I see that doesn't stop you from trying."

"Touché."

Jenna stood. "I'm sorry guys, I thought I lost her," Jenna mumbled. I reached behind Matt and grabbed her hand, attempting to let her know it was going to be okay.

"I wasn't following you," Gabriela spat. "I tracked lover boy over there through his cell phone. How do you think your girlfriend would react knowing you were spending time with your ex-wife?"

"Girlfriend?" I turned and glared at Matt. "The woman at your house–I'm sorry, *our* house–is your girlfriend?"

"Ali, don't." Matt's face reddened.

"Yes, his girlfriend, Allison," Gabriela said. "Matthew has moved on from you."

I turned toward Gabriela. Her lips curled up into a satisfied smile. Score one for Gabriela.

"So," Gabriela said as she flicked her fingernails, "what's going on here, huh? What's so damned important to you all–yes, you too Jenna as you're as much a member of this flock as Matt–risk sanctions from the Army for collaborating with the enemy?"

No one responded.

"Was this another one of Allison's futile attempts to win back Matt's heart? We know that's pointless."

I fisted my hands, attempting to stay calm. Here was yet another person dictating I couldn't see who I wanted. "Why you…" I lunged forward to attack when Matt stepped in front of me. His hands on my shoulders, he stared directly into my eyes. I studied his eyes and the mix of color that created those sweet hazels. Yellow spikes, green speckles and brown rings blurred together. My breath caught in my throat. My stomach flipped.

"Don't let her get to you," he whispered.

Matt turned and faced Gabriela. I straightened and attempted to relax.

"You don't control me, Gabriela," Matt said. "Quite frankly, it's none of your business what we're doing here. I'm a grown man and can do as I wish, see whoever I want. And as for Jenna, you know full well your declaration that Jenna is part of the flock was nothing more than conjecture. It doesn't change the fact she wasn't born an angel. She can see whomever she wants as well."

"Huh. Is that so? Is that what you think?" Gabriela stepped closer to Matt.

"Yes, absolutely," Matt responded confidently.

Gabriela cackled a high-pitched, uncomfortable laugh. "I see you have no respect for me, a senior member of Saint Michael's Army. You leave me no choice but to report your actions."

"Do it. Go ahead. Report whatever it is you think is going on here."

Gabriela was about to respond when the front door burst open and Vincent charged in.

"A party? And I wasn't invited?" Vincent asked sarcastically.

He and Gabriela stared each other down as he walked past her. Her lip snarled. Vincent ignored Matt as he passed, but Matt stepped into his path.

"You have no business being here," Matt said.

Vincent laughed. "And you do? Do you own this home, Matthew Carmichael? No, I don't believe you do. And you're no longer married to Allison, and considering you're an angel and she's a vampire, you are the one who has no business being here. I, at least, am dating Allison. I have more reason to be here than you."

"You asshole!" I shouted. "I told you yesterday I didn't want you here. I told you then to leave, but you don't listen. You're following me! Why are you following me? You have no right."

"Rights don't exist in our world, Allison."

Vincent went to step around Matt, but Matt matched his step and wouldn't allow it.

"Leave her alone," Matt demanded.

"Or what? What are you going to do, angel?"

Matt pulled his arm back, ready to strike. Gabriela, anticipating what was about to happen, leapt into action but was too late. Vincent picked Matt up with one hand and threw him across the room with the effort of pushing a piece of paper across a table. Matt crashed into the den doors and sprung to his feet. The sound of cloth tearing filled the air as Matt's wings sprung from his back. This was the first time I'd clearly seen him transform into the beautiful creature he was. His wings were nearly as tall as he, the tops curving just above his head, the tips barely brushing the ground. The wings fluffed before settling, errant feathers wafting to the floor. Vincent crouched, ready to fight. We women scampered to intervene as the rest of the Drakes came rushing through the front door.

"Well, I see we're right in the knick of time," Max observed.

"Knock it off, Vincent," Lorenzo demanded.

Gabriela rushed to Matt's side and whispered to him in another language, which Matt appeared to understand. He nodded but never broke eye contact with Vincent. Marlo grabbed Vincent's arm and shook him.

"What are you doing?" she asked.

He responded with a growl, still staring at Matt.

Gabriela continued coaxing Matt until his wings retreated.

Marlo shook Vincent's arm.

"What, sister?" he spat.

"What in the hell were you thinking, Vincent? Do you want to start a war?"

"Don't you see what's happening here? Don't any of you see what's happening here?"

The room was silent except for Vincent's labored breaths.

"These two," he pointed at Matt and me, "are meeting behind all of our backs. They're knowingly breaking the accord that states angels and vampires cannot comingle. Doesn't anyone care about rule and order anymore?"

"Of course we care," Lorenzo responded. "That's why we hurried here after you stormed out of the castle when Allison was leaving. Given she was at Matthew's house the other day and rushed off after that text we all assumed was from him, we suspected something might be going on and knew we needed to get here before you did something stupid, brother."

"Me? You accuse me of doing something stupid? What about you, brother? You're cavorting with an angel yourself. You're breaking one of the very rules you stand here now and say you're defending."

Lorenzo smirked and squared up to Vincent. "Now you just sound desperate. You know, as well as I do, that Jenna is not an angel. She wasn't born one, and no declaration in the world can change that.

Therefore, she and I seeing each other breaks no rules."

"What are you talking about?" Gabriela questioned.

Lorenzo walked to Jenna and they put their arms around each other.

"You two are seeing each other?" Gabriela asked. "But how? You've been sneaking around behind my back?"

Jenna responded with a smile.

The two of them made a cute couple, and their height difference was adorable. The top of Jenna's head met Lorenzo's bicep. Her long, flowing chocolate brown locks complemented his poker straight blond strands. Her olive toned skin looked bronzed next to his pallid complexion.

"Well this cannot be," Gabriella huffed. "I might be the only one here who agrees with Vincent; I believe in the enforcement of the rules. And it's clear plenty of rules have been broken and my repeated attempts to caution Matt and Allison have fallen on deaf ears. I have no choice but to report this to the Army."

"Do what you must," Lorenzo responded.

"Oh, not just Matt and Allison's actions," Gabriella continued. "I'll also be reporting Vincent's aggression toward Matthew."

"There was no harm done, Gabriela," Matt said. "No need to report this minor misunderstanding.""You don't get to tell me what I can and can't do. And likewise, I'll also be reporting your behavior, Lorenzo and Jenna. You put no stock in my declaration that Jenna is part of the flock, but I am a ranking member of the Army and have full authority to make such declarations."

"Fine, whatever, report what you must," Lorenzo said in a mocking tone. "And when we receive a subpoena for angel court, we'll be sure to show."

"You think this is funny, that this is a joke? This is a serious matter, and you'll find out how serious when the angels come knocking at your door. Let's go."

Gabriela stomped toward the front door. "The two of you—now!"

Matt walked over to me and whispered, "I'll take care of this. Nothing will be reported, okay?"

"Yeah, fine, take care of yourself. And Jenna, too."

"Will do." He gave me a half smile before turning on his heels and following Jenna out of the house.

Marlo closed the door and Vincent laid right into me.

"How dare you abandon your family when we need you the most."

"I didn't abandon you," I countered.

"It certainly appears that way," Max said.

"What are you talking about?"

"No sooner do you tell us you'll include us more in your investigation then you shoot down Marlo's offer to help and go rushing off as soon as you received a text. We can't afford distractions like this."

"This isn't a distraction, I swear. Did you all already forget what I said an hour ago at the castle? I didn't tell you about working with Matt because I knew you'd be against it. And I certainly couldn't have any of you come along with me to meet him as that surely would have scared him off."

Four unconvinced expressions glared at me.

"Look, Matt is helping me."

"Helping you with what, exactly?" Marlo asked. "We need more specifics."

I knew I had to say something to relieve the Drakes' suspicions that Matt and I were meeting for the sake of meeting, but I also knew I couldn't tell them too much. Felix's letter, after all, told me to trust no one, not even the Drakes.

"With Felix's murder," I muttered and looked down, suspecting the message wouldn't be well received because it wasn't specific enough.

"We already knew that," Vincent said.

"You need to be more forthright with what's actually going on," Max said.

Lorenzo crashed down on the couch, threw his arms over the back and stared at me.

"Because I thought he could help."

"Help? How could Matthew possibly help?" Lorenzo asked, agitation apparent in his voice.

"I thought maybe he might know something about the bullets used to kill Felix."

"And what made you think that?"

"I don't know. It was a hunch, something I thought worthy of exploring. Was there any harm in asking him the question? You all said you suspected the bullets were spelled. We know there are only two factions who are aware of the existence of vampires—angels and gypsies. In my mind, it made sense that one of them would be behind this. I obviously have an "in" with the angels given I was married to Matt, so I figured I'd give it a shot."

There was silence as everyone contemplated what I had said.

"Your logic makes sense," Max said. "And jives with what you said at the castle."

"Did Matthew know anything?" Vincent asked.

"No." I hoped I responded convincingly as I wasn't ready to reveal the truth. I didn't know where the truth would lead except to a fight at this point.

Vincent threw his arms in the air. "All this and he knew nothing."

"Hey, this is an investigation and at least we've crossed that off the list and can now focus elsewhere."

"Why not tell us in the first place, Allison?" Marlo asked.

"Tell you that I wanted to ask Matt about the bullets?"

"Yes."

"For fear of a reaction like this. I thought I could do it under the radar without causing such an ordeal, and if I had found something, then I surely would have brought it to you."

"I'm sorry, Allison," Lorenzo said.

I was taken aback by the apology. "Sorry? For what?"

"We shouldn't have jumped to conclusions without rationally confronting you about our suspicions." Lorenzo glared at Vincent who turned away.

"Thank you. Apology accepted."

"But you have to be more careful if you're going to take unsanctioned actions."

"I understand. And I promise, anything to do with Felix's murder investigation from here on out, I'll bring you into the loop first. Okay?"

There was a long pause before Lorenzo, Max and Marlo obliged. Vincent huffed and charged out the back door.

Chapter 13

Tall grasses stretch for as far as I can see. Shoulder height, the tan blades sway in the breeze. The wind sweeps over the field, rippling the grass like waves on an ocean. Straight ahead, the top of the field blends into the side of a hill. The abrupt end to the landscape indicates the land dips before rising back up into the hillside beyond. Pines, oaks and maples border the hill on both sides. There's not a cloud in the sky. The sun, high above, is a blinding ball of light. Through the rays, I see a kettle of buzzards circling as they float on air currents.

Inhaling, I smell the humid air of a hot summer's afternoon. A bead of sweat drips from my temple, and I wipe it with the back of my hand. Locusts intermittently rattle. Crickets chirp. I turn to look behind me and see more grass and trees. I glance up and see the buzzards have descended. Continuing to circle, I assume they're closing in on carrion for their evening meal.

I extend my arms in the air and twirl, enjoying the warmth of the sun on my skin. I close my eyes and listen to the insects, their sounds blending to form nature's chorus. The feather-like grass tickles my bare arms as I continue twirling until I drop to the ground sitting cross-legged. Looking up, the grass focuses my vision on the sky above, the only thing I can see from this angle. Suddenly something whizzes overhead. I hold my breath and concentrate on listening. I hear the noise again. It sounds like an arrow or bullet hissing through the air. I stand in an attempt to get a view of what might be going on. I stoop and cautiously peer through the fuzzy blooms on the tips of the grass. An object, small and fast, whirs by on my left, and then on my right. And then something hits the ground about ten feet in front of me, spraying chunks of dirt in my direction.

I run in the opposite direction from where the projectiles are coming. Multiple pounding footsteps race behind me. I turn and see the grass moving but can't see who's running in the field toward me. I trip over my foot and tumble to the ground. Hurrying to right myself, I will my legs to push through the pain but fail to stand. Blinded by the sun, I glance up and see two unidentifiable figures hovering above me pointing pistols.

My eyes sprang open and I gasped for air, my hair matted with sweat. It took me a moment to acclimate before realizing I'd been dreaming.

I straightened my legs and dropped from the ceiling beam–my new favorite resting spot. Landing on the living room floor, I thought to myself, just what I needed right now–another mysterious dream. The clock read 3:20 a.m. I felt well rested and decided my time would be better spent attempting to figure out what Felix's messages were telling me.

After showering and devouring three blood bags, I sat at the dining room table with a pad of paper and the clues I'd accumulated.

"Okay Felix. What are you trying to tell me?"

I smoothed out the creased clues: the couriered letter from Felix warning to trust no one and that the truth would find me, the Ulee clue I'd received from Mystery Vampire, the clue about my family tree found in my parents' crypt, and the X-marks-the-spot note found behind the painting at Castle Adena. I shuffled the notes, reordering them, but the resulting combinations made no sense.

"Felix, buddy, can you throw me a bone here?"

I got up and opened the curtains covering the back patio slider. Peering out the glass door, I observed the moon's reflection on the lake. A soft breeze rippled the water, distorting the image. The forest beyond wasn't fazed by the wind; trees stood tall and dark, motionless. My mind turned to Felix. What did I know about Felix that could help me figure out what he was trying to tell me? He was the technology guru of the Drake coven, but there was nothing technically savvy about the handwritten notes I'd received. These notes were old-school messages penned on paper. His interest in my lineage made it clear he had thoroughly enjoyed researching things. Unfortunately, the only thing research had to do with these clues was getting him killed and triggering the delivery of the messages. Felix also liked puzzles. His persistence studying the Bible Code—a big puzzle in and of itself—led to the discovery of clues which ultimately led me to Matt and to discovering where Jal and Lucious were attempting to access the Garden of Eden. Maybe this was some kind of puzzle I had to solve.

I sat back down and turned the legal pad long-ways. The couriered letter was delivered to my house, so I scrawled Ridge Hollow. The Ulee clue was given to me at the cemetery, the same place I had discovered the clue in my parents' crypt. I wrote down Riverside Cemetery. *X-marks-the-spot* was found at Castle Adena, and I wrote that name. I stared at the names of the three locations and wondered what they had in common. Felix had lived at Castle Adena and was now interred at Riverside Cemetery, but he had never lived in Ridge Hollow as far as I was aware.

I bit my pencil and decided to draw a rough outline of the state of

Ohio. I then plotted the three locations. Castle Adena and Riverside Cemetery appeared catty-corner on the map, so I drew a straight line between the locations.

"Okay, now what? There's not a fourth plot point to make an X."

I drew another straight line, starting at Ridge Hollow, crossing over the other line and extending it to the edge of the paper. Without an actual map, I had no idea what cities or landmarks might be plotted along the line, so that became my next mission.

Rummaging through a junk drawer was fruitless, as I didn't find anything useful to help me. But I found exactly what I was looking for in the garage. Though two years old, the atlas would serve its purpose. I flipped through the pages as I walked back into the house. I found the map of Ohio and laid the book open on the table, flattening the spine, forcing the book to stay open. I grabbed my pencil and quickly marked the three locations and drew the lines.

"Son of a peanut," I whispered when I realized I might have discovered the fourth location. But what did it mean?

"Come on Felix, you have to give me something more than that. Rattlesnake Island may be a small, private island, but it's as vast as an ocean if I don't know what I'm looking for."

Exhaling, I looked up and planned to get lost in the view of the forest again as I contemplated my discovery. But the thought was short lived once I saw mist outside of the glass door. Normally, I might have attributed the mist to cool night air settling on the warm ground, but the mist was outside only one of the glass panes. As I watched, the window fogged and a message appeared one letter at a time:

Answers you seek

Not all in your tree

Found within the Flock

If your curiosity I pique
Go to what's home for me
Find a key to truth unlock

"What in the heck is this?" I rubbed my eyes to ensure I was seeing clearly, and I certainly was. But I had to read fast because the fogged message disappeared as the next line appeared. I scribbled what I saw without taking my eyes off the door.

I waited a few seconds to see if the message would continue, and when it didn't, I ran to the door and yanked on the handle. The door didn't budge even though I knew I had unlocked it. "Damn it," I cursed as I remembered the safety lock embedded in the frame. I reached up and pulled the lever down, yanking the door open. The mist was gone, and no one was in sight. I closed my eyes and breathed in the night air but didn't detect a scent. I extended my hearing and identified the faint rustle of leaves but nothing else. There was only one person I knew who could vanish into thin air. Mystery Vampire was here… and now he was gone.

Chapter 14

D awn was breaking on the horizon, a slight glow against the last bit of nightfall. Stars twinkled in the night sky like lights on a switchboard. A sliver of moon pierced the darkness to the west, saying its final goodbye to this part of the world for this night.

I sped through the woods, leaping over fallen trees, charging through brush and occasionally leaping from branch to branch. A symphony of creatures serenaded the night, their performance uninterrupted as I moved so fast they didn't even know I was there. I slowed as I approached Matt's backyard.

Separating the evergreens with my hands, I peered at the back of the house. All of the lights were out, so I assumed everyone was still asleep. A quick glance at the driveway told me Little Miss Booty Call wasn't here tonight. *Perfect*, I thought to myself.

I dashed across the backyard, leapfrogging the fire pit, stopping when I arrived at the garage doors. I quickly surveyed the area to ensure I was still alone before slinking along the side of the garage and rounding the corner. I tiptoed through mulch beds, careful to make as little noise as possible. I arrived at the corner and turned, walking toward the front of the house where the garage met the front of the home. I hopped up, one leg on the brick garage, the other on the stucco face of the house, and climbed Spiderman-like. Ten hops later and I was at the gutter, the second floor window to Matt's bedroom a short leap to my right. I positioned my body for the jump, mustered the energy and spring-boarded off the house, twisting in the air. My fingers clutched the wood window frame. My feet found a piece of wood on the Tudor border that was barely wide enough for me to balance. I waited a moment to confirm I had my footing, then extended my index finger and gingerly tapped the glass in a five beat cadence. Seconds passed and I didn't hear any movement, so I tapped again but with more urgency.

"Come on, Matt," I whispered. My biceps burned from supporting most of my weight. My legs quivered, attempting to maintain balance on the one-inch thick wood border. Right about now, I wished I had the supernatural gift of levity so I could float while I waited. I tapped again, as I noticed a gap in the horizontal blinds. Matt's eyes widened when he saw me. My right elbow propped on the border, I gave a smile and a brief wave.

He lifted the blinds quietly yet with urgency, then unlocked the window and cranked it open. He rubbed his eyes with one hand. "Allison? What in the world are you doing here? Do you know what time it is?" He looked over his shoulder at the alarm clock.

I ogled and internally salivated at the sight of a shirtless Matt. He had most definitely been hitting the gym harder in the past months and the results were drool worthy. My foot lost traction as I watched his back muscles flex as he turned back to face me. He had gotten a new tattoo too. I only caught a glimpse of the artwork on his left shoulder; it was round, resembling a shield, with a cross in the middle surrounded by rivets. Two swords made an X behind the shield and wings extended from both sides.

"Whoa, whoa, whoa." Matt removed the screen and extended a hand to me. "How in the world are you hanging on out there?"

I grabbed his hand as he poked his head outside to see how I was braced.

"It's those vampire agilities," I quipped.

Our cheeks brushed as Matt settled himself on the window seat.

"It looks like you could use a hand," he joked. My right hand locked with his left, and he grabbed my arm with his right hand. He leaned out the window, as I wasn't able to cross the windowsill due to the impenetrable force preventing a vampire from entering an archangel's home.

"We really have to do something about this," I said as I inclined my head toward the windowsill.

"I'd love to sit here and chit chat, but um, the sun is rising and Gabriela will be up soon. What are you doing here, Allison?"

"I found another clue."

"You what? Where? What did the clue say?"

"Well I guess you could say the clue kind of found me."

Matt waited for me to continue. "I couldn't rest this morning, so I got up and decided to work on all of the clues we've found so far. I started thinking about Felix and his fondness for puzzles and figured I'd better start connecting some dots or we're never going to figure out what Felix discovered."

"Ali, I hate to cut you short, but you need to get to the point." Matt looked over my shoulder at the rising sun.

"Okay, well this mist appeared outside my sliding door and the next thing I know, a message was being written on the fogged glass."

"What? Who was there?"

"I assume it was Mystery Vampire as he's the only one I know who can turn into mist. But I had no time to figure it out since the message faded as soon as it appeared. I hurried to write it down, and by the time I finished and fumbled with the door, he—assuming it was him—was long gone."

"What did the message say?"

"It was a poem."

"A poem?"

"Or maybe a riddle, something about the answers aren't all in my tree but can be found within the flock and there's an additional clue, a key to be exact. If you reach into my pocket," I nudged my head toward my pants pocket, "you can read it for yourself."

Without hesitating, Matt leaned out the window and used one hand to reach into my pocket. His neck close to my face, I took advantage of the situation and inhaled his scent. I drew the muskiness deep into my lungs, wishing I could bottle his fragrance and take it with me.

Matt settled back onto the window seat, still grasping my arm as he unfolded the piece of paper and read the poem.

"Is this alluding to his murder or your lineage?"

"I'm guessing my lineage. I know where to look for this key."

"You do? How?"

I let out a hefty sigh. "You know I'm supposed to be helping the Drakes find Felix's killer."

"Yeah, and?"

"Well they seem a bit suspicious that I haven't been helping too much with the investigation, at least in their eyes. I mean I don't know what they expected given we've been planning Felix's funeral. I figured our investigation would gear up right around now, after the funeral. I suspect Vincent might be feeding into their fears that I'm doing more with you than just trying to solve a murder."

"They know we're working together?"

"Yeah, long story. The Ruling Council knows too.""Ali!"

"Matt, I had to. It was the only way to diffuse the situation. Anyway, as soon as I received this clue, I called Marlo. I'd promised her and the brothers I'd be more inclusive of them in my sleuthing, so I figured what better way than to ask about where Felix considered home."

"Wasn't she slightly suspicious when you told her about this mysterious clue?"

"No, because I didn't tell her. I played it off thinking maybe there would be clues at the place Felix considered home, some place besides the castle."

"And?"

"Marlo said Felix has a place on Rattlesnake Island. He much preferred it up there because of the seclusion. He'd lock himself away and spend weeks deciphering the latest puzzle or code or building his latest gadget. I'm willing to bet he might have left another clue there."

"All right. So let's go to Rattlesnake Island."

I smiled. "I like the way you think, but I'll be making this trip solo."

"What? No. Ali, I'll go with you."

"As much as I appreciate the offer, I can't take you. Matt, you've heard the rumors about the island. I can confirm most are true. You can't get on the island unless you've been vetted, and you haven't been. Plus, it would raise all sorts of bells and whistles if I got caught sneaking an archangel onto the vampires' private island."

"I guess you're right, but I don't like this. I'm worried about you.""Don't be. I've been on the island before; I have every right to be there."

"It's not that. What if someone, something…"

"Matt, look at me." His hazel eyes met my gaze and instantly made my stomach tickle. "I can take care of myself." I nodded my head.

He exhaled. "Yeah, I know. But if you didn't come here to ask me to go with you, why'd you stop by?"

"I didn't want to call or text given recent events. And I wanted someone to know where I was going."

"Ali," Matt began to plead.

"Hey," I said, "blame this on yourself and my overprotective parents. All three of you always told me to make sure someone knew where I was going 'just in case.'"

"I don't like this."

"You don't have to like it. Besides, I also wanted to see if you got any farther with my family tree."

"I've been working on it, but nothing yet. I'd be farther along if Jenna would help more."

"She's still sneaking around with Lorenzo?"

"Yep, even more so given Lorenzo's declaration to Gabriela at your house. She sleeps most days away since she's spending all night with him."

"Hmm, she sounds like a vampire," I joked. "Any way to try to get her to focus on this for a few days?"

"You'd like that wouldn't you? To get her away from Lorenzo?"

"Hey, Lorenzo is a great guy, but I'm still not comfortable with my best friend dating a vampire."

"Really? But you're a vampire and I'm..."

"And we're no longer married, remember?"

"Uh, yeah. Hey," he cleared his throat. "I discovered something else."

"What's that?"

"I plotted on a map the locations of where all the clues were found."

"So did I."

"Really? Here, hang on." Matt placed my hands on the sill. "Got that?"

"Yeah." I clung to the wood as Matt scampered to the dresser. He pulled open a drawer and quickly closed it. He ran back to the window seat and grabbed my arms to assist me while unfolding the map with one hand and his mouth.

"Great minds, right?" Matt joked. "So then you know that for the clues we have, if you draw an X through them —"

"The fourth plot point would be Rattlesnake Island."

"No. What?"

I struggled to prop my elbow while attempting to point at the map. Drawing a line with my finger, I illustrated that Rattlesnake Island completed the X.

"Well that's interesting," Matt said. "I was so focused on where the lines intersected that I didn't think about the missing point."

"Where do the lines intersect?" I craned my neck to get a better look at the map.

"Buzzard's Roost."

"That's awfully interesting given Felix's body was discovered in the area."

"Have you been there?" Matt asked.

"No, but Marlo found Felix there and she and Max have gone back. They didn't find anything."

"Did they search the whole area? That field is enormous."

"I don't know specifically where they looked besides the area immediately around where Marlo found Felix."

"Well maybe Jenna and I can head out there and check it out. It can't be a coincidence. And with this last clue, Rattlesnake Island would complete the grid. There has to be a clue there, Ali."

"Maybe. How about this? You and Jenna work on the family tree and if you have time, head out to Buzzard's Roost. Maybe I can even meet you there later after I return from Rattlesnake Island. The three of us can put our heads together and try to solve this."

"Sounds good."

I smiled and then looked down, preparing to jump.

"Ali?""Yeah?"

I turned my head and wasn't expecting Matt to be right there, our noses almost colliding. He pecked my cheek. His soft lips lingered on my skin, sending an electrified wave throughout my body. I slowly pulled my head back, our faces close. His warm breath hit my face with each breath he took. If I could have freed a hand to grab him and pull him close and press those lips to mine, I would have.

"Be careful," he whispered.

I would have given anything to have read his mind at that exact moment.

"I will."

Matt surveyed the ground below. "You got this?"

"Yeah, no problem." I released his hand and fell, landing without making a sound. I looked back up. Matt was replacing the screen and mouthed, "Be careful."

I smiled and mouthed, "Of course."

Of course I'd be careful; I needed to figure out what that kiss meant.

Chapter 15

The jet ski skidded to a halt on the shoreline, sand crunching beneath the fiberglass exterior. Grabbing a handle, I gave the machine a quick pull to get it out of the surf. No sooner had I set foot on the island when two armed vampire guards greeted me. I raised my hands defensively.

"Good morning, gentlemen," I called out.

The shorter one stopped two feet in front of me. What he lacked in stature, he made up for with the firepower he carried. Bullets crisscrossed his chest; some sort of rifle was flung over one shoulder and he carried handguns on both hips and one strapped to his thigh. He scanned my face, hopefully seeing the thirteen flecks in my eyes. He sniffed the air. "Allison Carmichael?"

"That's me."

The taller guard wore more tattoos than clothing. He feverishly typed something into his phone. "It's her," he confirmed.

"We don't have record of your scheduled arrival."

"That's because I didn't schedule this trip."

"You are familiar with our protocol, correct?"

I sighed. "Yes, I'm familiar with your protocol, but sometimes protocol doesn't correspond with a spontaneous visit. I was out and about this morning, found myself at the marina and figured I'd take a jet ski out for a spin and ended up here. I hope that's not a problem. I mean, I know I've been vetted previously."

Rambo eyed me suspiciously.

"She's good," the other said as he flashed the phone to his buddy. Shorty looked at the phone and back at me.

"Where you headed?"

"Um, I don't think I have to answer that. You see that I'm permitted to be on the island and where I plan to go should be of no concern."

"Um," the guard mocked, "had you informed us of your visit, you would have had to have told us where you were going, so I think it is a valid question."

"Fair enough." I didn't want to raise their suspicions any more than they were already. But I also didn't want everyone to know I was headed to Felix's cottage. I figured the fewer people who knew, the better. "I'm headed to Vincent's cabin."

"Really?" The two guards looked at each other. "Does Vincent know that?"

"Probably not since this visit wasn't planned. It's not a problem, is it? I mean I have been to his place before."

"No, no a problem at all.""Okay then."

I walked between them and started heading west when one of the guards called out to me.

"What is it?"

"Vincent's cabin is that way." He pointed east.

Crap, I thought. I had started walking in the direction of Felix's cottage. I quickly looked around as if trying to recalibrate my internal compass. "Ah, yeah, thanks. Sorry, I was never very good with directions."

I turned east and thanked him again for correcting me. Once I got to the interior of the island and was confident the guards weren't following, I headed towards Felix's.

Marlo had given me directions when we spoke earlier. At first she had insisted on meeting me and helping search Felix's home, but I told her I had it under control and she should focus on figuring out what enemies Felix might have had. We could catch up later and I could fill her in on anything I'd found. That would be my good faith attempt to include her in my search and findings.

I approached the cottage and looked over my shoulder. Although I didn't expect anyone to be there, one couldn't be too cautious. The cottage appeared locked up and all the lights were off. I stayed close to the tree line on the outskirts of the property before running across the yard, looking over both shoulders. A few steps from the front porch, I detected a familiar scent. I slowed my pace, lifted my head to the sky and shook it. You had to be kidding me. *Damn it, Marlo.* She had sold me out. Hopping onto the porch, I noticed the door was ajar so I pushed it open and stepped inside. Vincent was sitting on the couch leafing through papers sprawled out on the table.

"I'm surprised to see you here," I said.

He looked up, a cocky expression on his face like he'd been expecting me. "Marlo mentioned you called earlier and were asking about this place. I figured I'd help you search for clues."

Sure you did, I thought. "I told Marlo I'd check it out myself and report back to her later."

"I know you did. She told me that too."

"And yet here you are."

Vincent stood. "Is there a reason you wanted to be here alone?"

"No," I quickly replied, deflecting his suspicions. "I just thought Marlo would have trusted me enough to handle this on my own."

"She trusts you."

"But you don't?"

"It's not that, Allison. Why must you be so adamant about doing everything on your own? Why can't you accept help once in awhile?"

"I don't know. Maybe because the last time you tried helping me I ended up in vampire rehab for 66 torturous days."

"Allison, this is different." Vincent walked to me and grabbed my arms. "We all have the same goal this time. We want to find Felix's killer and bring him to justice."

"Mmm hmm."

"What do you want from me, huh? I've apologized a million times about tricking you into returning to the castle. And every time I think we're good, we're not. I've done nothing but try to help you since your recovery. I've been trying to help you figure out your dream, but you keep shutting me out. I'm trying to help you search for clues about my brother's killer, but you're shutting me out here, too."

I drew a deep breath and felt the sting of tears I didn't want to spill. A pit of confusion knotted my stomach. I didn't know what I wanted from Vincent, but I couldn't keep this act up. It wasn't fair to Vincent, and it simply wasn't me. My parents had raised me to treat people better than I had been treating Vincent.

"Vincent, I'm the one that needs to apologize."

He flinched at my admission.

"I know, right. Allison apologizing?"

"I wasn't expecting you to—"

"Why would you? I've treated you like crap these past few months. I tell myself that I've come to terms with the fact I consented to my transformation, yet deep down, I still blame you despite seeing the video that clearly recorded my consent."

"Allison—"

"No, don't Vincent. This is long overdue. I blame you for

everything that happened after that too—me running away attempting life on my own only to end up with a severe addiction to human blood. And my blame doesn't stop there. I hold it against you that you tricked me into returning to the States but don't hold Max to the same standard when you both were accountable for forcing me into rehab, which I clearly needed, though I failed to see it at the time. Vincent, you've been my scapegoat for everything that has been wrong in my life in the past year. That was so very wrong of me and I am sorry. Can you ever forgive me?" Adrenaline coursed through my body, fueling my confession. When the last word passed my lips, I felt lightheaded from the mix of emotions—relief, remorse and satisfaction in having done the right thing.

Vincent whistled and ran a hand through his hair. "Wow. I wasn't expecting this, Allison. Of course I forgive you. I love you."

The words were like a sucker punch to my stomach. He rarely said those words to me. I certainly wasn't going to reciprocate. I couldn't lead him on like that.

"Vincent, I—"

"Stop. You don't have to say anything else." It was almost as if he knew what I was about to say, what I was about to do, and didn't want to hear it. "It has been a difficult year for you, and I'm not here to pressure you into anything. I'm trying to help you, if you'll let me. I've loved you for such a long time. I'd do anything for you."

I closed my eyes. I needed to break things off with Vincent, and although the words swirled in my head, I couldn't collect them into a coherent sentence, never mind a single word. "You've loved me for a long time?" I whispered. The phrase was the only thing I had latched onto in his last statement.

"Yes, but don't you know that by now? As I watched you grow into the beautiful woman you've become, I've fallen head over heels in love with you. I've waited this long for you; I can wait a little bit longer."

My heart sank. Vincent sounded so sincere, but were his words truthful? Did he truly love me for me, or did he love the idea of me–the first descendant transformed into a vampire, just another trophy to add to his collection? Even if it were the latter, that was still love to Vincent. He had me reeling emotionally. I wasn't in the proper state of mind to attempt a break up, and this wasn't the place to do it. I had envisioned doing it in a public place so Vincent couldn't cause a scene and I could escape. I stared blankly, unsure of what to do next.

Vincent cleared his throat, breaking the silence. "So, um, how'd you think to search this place? Did your dream lead you here?"

"No."

"Have you figured out what your dream means?"

There he went again with the dream. Why was he so desperate to know if I'd deciphered that mystery? "Ah, no," I lied. Even after our heart-to-heart, I wasn't giving up that secret yet. Felix's letter had warned to trust no one, and until I figured out what that meant and who I could and couldn't trust, I was going to keep all secrets close to me. "It was a hunch, that's all. I figured if this was a place Felix spent most of his time, then maybe there'd be a clue here."

"It's a good idea. Any hunches on where to begin?"

We circled the floor, taking in the space. There were more laptops and desktops than any one person needed. A map of the States was clipped on a drawing board while a map of the island was pinned to a corkboard above it. I flipped on a light in the spare room which was filled with green circuit boards, tiny resistors, capacitors, soldering equipment and other tools.

"I haven't the slightest idea where to begin in all this. Haven't you been here before? Where would you begin?"

"Our personal cottages were just that–personal. A place for us to escape when we needed solitude. I haven't been here just as my siblings haven't been to my cottage."

"All right then. I can tell you that I'm not going to have the patience to look through that." I pointed into the electronics den. Vincent peeked into the room and chuckled.

"Good old Felix, always tinkering with something. How about this? I'll take this room and his bedroom. You start out here."

"Sounds like a plan to me."

Vincent started with Felix's bedroom. I couldn't blame him as the electronics room looked to be a tedious task. He shook the windows and yelled that they were locked and hadn't been tampered with. I started with the maps. I flipped through multiple oversized sheets of paper but didn't spot any scribbling or other obvious clues. Bending down, I examined a short tower of drawers and pulled open each one only to find stacks of blank stationary, pens and other office supplies. I paused when I found Felix's wax seal. I inspected it for no other reason than the last time I saw the seal was on the note left at my parents' crypt. I envisioned Felix sitting in the chair, penning the note, pressing the object to the envelope, wax pooling around it.

"Dammit Felix; what are you hiding for me here?" I muttered.

"Did you find something?" Vincent leaned against the doorframe.

"No." I dropped the seal in the drawer and pushed it shut.

"Well keep looking, we have plenty more ground to cover."

I paced the kitchen as Vincent returned to the bedroom, closing the door so he could access the closet.

I randomly opened kitchen cabinets, not sure what I should be looking for.

"Think, Allison, think."

I thought of the poem. If your curiosity I pique, go to what's home for me, find a key to truth unlock.

I was looking for a key, but was I looking for a key in the literal sense of the word? I pulled open another drawer. It was brimming with sticky notes, pens, tape, tacks—a junk drawer, somewhere that I'd normally place spare keys. I rifled through the contents, but there was nothing of interest.

Slamming the drawer, I leaned my hip against the counter and growled. I cracked my neck to relieve the stress that was constricting my muscles when something caught my eye. I stepped around the corner to get a better view of the entryway and what hung on the wall—a key holder in the shape of a key. *Very funny, Felix.* The skeleton key-shaped wall mount was tarnished and had three hooks. The keys to his BMW hung on one, a round metal object dangled from the middle hook, and a key shaped like the wall decoration was on the third. I touched the round object, turning it over, and noticed ornate scrollwork around the circumference. The engraving reminded me of the etching on Felix's sarcophagus. I glanced at the key hanging next to it and thought that this was too easy. Would Felix have left a clue hanging for me in plain sight?

I plucked both objects off the hooks and held one in each hand, gingerly bouncing them as if determining which weighed more. The key appeared to be the obvious clue based on the riddle. The message that had appeared on my glass door indicated that I'd find a key that would unlock the truth. But what I didn't know was what specifically the key was supposed to unlock that would reveal the truth. I rotated the metal object, uncertain what it was. Although no keyhole was present, I felt the engraving too much of a coincidence to overlook. Running a finger over the design, I discovered a small square button. The lid popped when I pushed the button, revealing a compass. I watched as the dial spun as the device calibrated. *Great*, I thought. I had a hard enough time with directions as it was; I had no idea how to use a compass. And besides, what in the heck was the compass even for? Rattlesnake Island was so small that I couldn't imagine Felix needing it to navigate here. And didn't I need plot points for this thing to lead me somewhere? On top of that, was the key also part of the clue and if so, what did it unlock? Maybe a container of some sort concealing coordinates that I assumed I needed for the compass.

"Allison?"

"Huh? What?" I closed the compass lid and slid it in one pocket, placing the key in the other.

"I asked how it was going out here."

"Oh, um, not well. I haven't found a single thing." I leaned against the wall and lost my balance, my arm knocking into the key holder. A piece of paper wafted to the floor.

"What's that?" Vincent asked as he approached.

"Not sure." I hurried to scoop it up before he got to it. It was a ripped piece of paper with a map on one side. On the back, "Riverside Cemetery" was in bold letters. As I scanned through the marketing material, my eyes did a double take when I read the tag line about them serving as your final home, your final resting spot. *Go to what's home for me.* Could Felix have been telling me there was another clue at the cemetery, specifically at his grave, his final resting spot? "It's, um, part of a brochure for Riverside."

"That fell out from behind the key holder?"

Vincent walked over and tugged on the wall mount, ripping out part of the wall, drywall dust falling to the floor.

"Was that necessary?" I asked.

Vincent looked at the back of the decoration and the hole he had created in the wall.

"What were you expecting?" I asked.

"I don't know. Anything was possible with my brother. I thought maybe he'd have hidden some papers behind here or something."

I shrugged.

"You didn't find anything else out here?" he asked.

"Nope. Not a thing."

"There are three hooks but only one is used. There was nothing on the other two?"

I shook my head.

"Well then, I guess it's back at it. There was nothing in his bedroom so I'll move over to this room." Vincent pointed to the room with the electronics components.

"I'll, um, keep looking over here," I pointed over my shoulder.

"Yeah, sounds good. With the both of us here, it shouldn't take that much longer to go through this place."

"Mmm hmm," I responded with a nod.

Vincent walked into the spare room and as soon as I heard him rummaging through drawers, I snuck out the front door.

Chapter 16

Back on the mainland, the first thing I did was call Matt. "Matt," I huffed into the phone.

"Ali? Did you find anything at Felix's house?"

"Yeah, Vincent."

"I can barely hear you. Where are you?"

I slowed to a jog in order to reduce the wind noise.

"Sorry about that. I'm heading to my next destination."

"Did you find anything at Felix's?"

"Yeah, Vincent was there. Apparently Marlo thought I could use the help and Vincent was more than happy to volunteer."

"Are they on to you?"

"I don't know. I think they think something is up but they can't put a finger on it."

"Did you find anything?"

"I sure did."

"What is it?"

"I'm not sure, but I think Felix left another clue."

"Oh come on, another clue?"

"Two clues to be exact. Can you meet at the cemetery?"

"Absolutely." There was a pause. "Ali, I found something too."

I stopped jogging as a shiver traveled down my spine. "Is it about my family tree?"

"I'll tell you when I see you."

"Matt, tell me now."

"I have to go. Gabriela is here. I'll see you at the cemetery." He disconnected the call.

I stared at the phone for a few seconds as if that would get me the answer sooner. I shoved the phone in my pocket and took off at warp vampire speed to get to the cemetery.

The man sitting at the bus stop kept glancing at me as I paced in front of the locked main gate at Riverside Cemetery. I turned on my heels and caught him as he looked away. I pulled out my phone and checked it a few times to give the appearance that I was waiting for someone. I don't know why I felt compelled to care what this man thought of me. If he wanted to give me any trouble, I'd simply break his neck. Or sink my fangs in it.

"Ali-gator," Matt wheezed as he approached.

"You ran here?"

Matt doubled over and put his hands on his knees to catch his breath. "Of course not. I parked around the block, thinking it better to keep my car off the main road."

"Ah, good call. Want me to give you a lift over the fence?"

"What?"

"You look tired, that's all. And the fence is locked since the cemetery isn't open yet."

"You seem to forget that you're not the only one with supernatural abilities." Matt looked over both shoulders as if preparing to do something.

"Wait," I shouted. "You can't."

"What? Why not?"

"There's a guy sitting at the bus stop." I looked beyond Matt but the bus stop was empty. Matt looked as well. "Well that's strange.""What's that?"

"There was a guy sitting there the whole time I was here." I pointed across the street at the wooden bench surrounded by glass on three sides.

"Well he's not there now."

"Yeah, but I didn't hear a bus drive by, did you?"

"Come on, Ali. We can't sit here and debate things like this. Vincent is on to you, Gabriela is on to me, and who knows about your new buddy Lucretia."

"You're right. Let's get to Felix's grave. It's two sections north from my parents' crypt." I pointed in the general direction.

Matt smiled a mischievous little grin.

"What is it?"

His wings ripped through his shirt. With one leap, he was in the air on his way over the wrought iron gate. I smiled at the sight of my husband, rather my former husband. His wings flapped without effort, the silky white feathers catching the rising sun. He zipped through the trees.

"Game on, Mr. Carmichael," I said to myself. I took two steps and leapt to the top of the fence, momentarily landing with my right foot between two sharp points before leaping to the ground and running after Matt.

"Beat you," Matt joked as I slowed, stopping at Felix's tomb. Matt's wings receded.

"Only because I let you."

Matt laughed me off. "So what are we looking for?"

"Not sure. But I think Felix wanted me to come here. Look at this."

I pulled out the ripped leaflet and pointed to the tag line.

"Final home, huh?"

"I think it's too much of a coincidence that the message on my door referenced what is home to him and then I find this at his house."

"Really? I mean if the guy was planning his funeral, is it uncommon for him to have a cemetery pamphlet at his house?"

"It wouldn't, but it is odd that it was tucked behind a wall mounted key holder with this." I pulled the compass and key from my pocket.

"What is that?" Matt walked closer and placed a hand behind the compass as I dangled it and the key.

"This is a key," I joked as I bounced the key.

Matt looked at me as if to say, really?

"It's a compass. But that's not the interesting part. Look at the scrollwork on the side."

Matt rotated the object, squinting his eyes as he examined the design that ran along the seam.

"Look familiar?" I asked as I nudged my head in the direction of Felix's sarcophagus.

"Now that I don't think is a coincidence. It's the same design." Matt dragged his hand over the Celtic design bordering the cement tomb. "But what does the design on the compass," he pointed back to the trinket in my hand, "have to do with his tomb? And what about the key?"

"Both good questions."

"Here, let me see that." Matt grabbed the compass and popped it open. "This is strange."

"What's that?"

"This compass isn't aligning to True North."

"What does that mean?"

"When you open a compass, you see how it swivels around? It's trying to align itself with the earth's rotation and once it stops, the arrow should point to True North. But that would be about that way." Matt extended his arm in front of him. "And this is pointing that way." Matt extended his other arm in the opposite direction.

"So what does that mean?"

"I wonder if Felix tinkered with this to point us, I mean you, in the direction of something he wants you to find. But coordinates sure would be helpful."

"Well do you think coordinates could be here?"

"I don't know." Matt looked around, taking in the tombstone before his eyes settled on the sarcophagus. "Was this inscribed before or after his funeral?"

"It was done before. I remember seeing the lid off to the side at the service already carved."

"Well Ali, I don't know. I guess we look and see if anything catches our attention."

"Huh," I mused.

"What is it?" Matt straightened and followed my gaze.

"Well something caught my attention, but I don't think it's what we're looking for." I pointed to the grave marker that stood about a foot in front of the tomb. The three foot high chunk of gray marble was topped with a flock of angels sitting amongst clouds. Some held horns, while others reached toward the sky in reflection. A dragon, what I presumed symbolized the Devil, loomed below the clouds, angels stepping on its head preventing it from getting to the cloud. Below that on the smooth surface, DRAKE was etched in large letters, and underneath that, Felix's name, date of birth, and date of death.

"According to this," Matt said, "Felix was only thirty-five years old."

I giggled. "Yeah, give or take a couple thousand years. But that is Felix's actual month and day of birth." Of course Felix couldn't have used the actual year of his birth. It would have drawn attention and questions that neither the Drakes nor the Ruling Council would have been pleased with. But there was something unsettling to me about Felix being buried in a tomb with incorrect information on his headstone, almost as if it were a lie or a sham for the rest of the world. It also wasn't fair to Felix to have to be buried with false information, having to continue this farce even in death, protecting the existence of immortals. I sighed as there was nothing that could be done about it.

"Come on," Matt urged, "we have to get moving."

"Yeah, you're right."

Matt walked around the grave marker. I bent to eye level, checking out the cement tomb. I slid both hands along the edge, my fingers rippling over the engraving. I turned the corner around the front of the tomb and stopped when I made the next turn.

"Matt."

"What is it?" Matt jogged over to my side.

"Look at this." I pointed to a series of numbers etched between alternating peaks in the scrollwork. Forty-one appeared first, followed by a space filled with tiny circles, followed by 21501. Several spaces later, there was an -81, followed by more circles, then 70976 in the following five spaces. I pulled out my phone and took pictures as Matt scanned the rest of the perimeter for more numbers.

"What do you think it is?" I asked.

"Ingenious."

"What? You know what the numbers represent?"

I detected a familiar scent and it stopped me dead in my tracks. Before I could warn Matt, I heard Vincent's voice.

"I absolutely know what this means," Vincent retorted.

"Oh shit," Matt muttered. He walked to my side as Vincent marched toward us.

"Vincent—" I started.

"Don't." He stopped at the foot of Felix's tomb, glancing first at the monument and then at Matt and me. He opened his mouth several times as if to say something, but closed it each time. "You've been lying to me, Allison, and to your family." He cracked his knuckles and neck, looking side-to-side as if the sight of Matt and I disgusted him. "Your apology to me earlier, was that a farce? Did you mean any of it or did you simply utter those words hoping to throw me off track? You know, I've been more than patient with you, Allison, as you've gone through this transition and detox and adjusted to your existence as a vampire. But enough is enough. You damn well know that you," he stuck his index finger in my face, "cannot be hanging around with angels yet you keep doing it. Now tell me, what in the world have the two of you been up to and what are you doing here now?"

"The same question could be asked of you," a female voice said.

"Oh Jesus," I whispered.

Vincent rolled his eyes. "Lucretia," he yelled. "Show yourself."

"So testy," Lucretia chided as she emerged from behind a tombstone resembling a miniature Washington monument. "Is there a reason that you're on edge, hmm? Is it because the love of your life is here with the love of her life? Oh wait; it can't be that. Love would imply that you have emotions, and I know better than anyone that you're not capable of feeling anything for anyone but yourself."

"What do you want?" Vincent growled.

Matt and I exchanged glances and tried to not make a sound.

Lucretia laughed. "Oh Vincent, dear, you know what I want. I've already told you. And by following you two around," she waved a hand between Vincent and me, "I'll figure things out before you know it."

"You followed me here?"

"I followed Allison to Rattlesnake Island and then yes, I followed you here. No sense in following her when I knew you'd be hot on her trail. I didn't want you picking up my scent, you know?"

"Why you–" Vincent lunged at Lucretia but with one fell swoop, she knocked him to the ground.

"Why me what, Vincent? Huh? What are you going to do to me?" She ground the heel of her boot into his back. "Are you going to try to stop me? Are you going to try to silence me? That's not going to happen. I'm getting close to figuring out what you've been hiding, what you've been up to. And once I do, I'm going to expose you for the snake that you are."

"Talk about an ex-girlfriend scorned," Matt whispered to me.

"What did you say, angel?"

"Darn it, Matt, vampire hearing," I whispered.

Lucretia stepped over Vincent, sinking all of her weight into his back, and slinked toward us.

"What exactly, are you two lovebirds doing here?" She looked at my phone and then back at me. "Why don't you save us all the time and just tell me what you found. You know I'm going to find out sooner or later."

Lucretia charged me, her arm outstretched, hand reaching for my phone. Matt wrapped his arm around my waist, circling the other around my back, and the next thing I knew we were flying through the air. It took a moment for my mind to catch up with the flurry of activity, but the whooshing of air filling my ears as Matt's wings flapped made me realize he'd sprung his wings and sprung us from what could have been a very bad situation. I looked down between Matt's wings and saw Vincent and Lucretia toe to toe, fists waving in the air. That was one fight I was happy to not be part of.

About a minute later and several city blocks away from the cemetery, Matt and I landed on a rooftop of a commercial building.

"Well that was interesting," I said.

"Yeah, I didn't want to stick around and see what Lucretia had in store for us."

"Um, not that."

"Oh," Matt quipped. "Your first time flying?" His wings receded.

"With an angel? Yes."

Matt smiled as he pulled his phone from his pocket.

"Who are you calling?" I asked.

"Jenna."

"For what?"

"Do you know what those numbers are?"

"Not a clue."

"They're latitude and longitude coordinates."

"How do you know that?"

"It's how the Army keeps track of all descendants. They've plotted where they all live."

"What do you think the coordinates are for? Something to do with the compass?"

"I have a hunch, and if Jenna ever picks up, we'll find out. Hey, Jenna, no time to explain. Are you near a computer? Okay, you need to search the web for a page that plots latitude and longitude coordinates. Here, jot these numbers down and call me as soon as you get a location." Matt grabbed my phone, pulled up the pictures and recited the numbers. "Hurry, Jenna. We have some pissed off vampires on our tails." Matt disconnected the call.

"Why don't they make smart throw away phones?" Matt asked as he waved the generic burner I'd given him the day before.

"I'm sorry," I said.

"Hey." Matt walked over and placed a hand on my chin. "You didn't do anything wrong. In fact, good call on your part figuring out people were using our cell phones to track us. These throw away phones bought us some time."

Tears brimmed in my eyes.

"I take it you weren't apologizing about the phones?"

I shook my head.

"What's going on, Ali?"

I lifted my head to look at Matt and tears spilled from my eyes. I quickly wiped my cheeks before the venom seared my skin. I took a couple of deep breaths.

"I'm sorry for everything I've put you through."

"What? What are you talking about?"

"Everything over the past year. It's all been my fault. I'm sorry for the pain I've caused you."

"None of this is your fault."

"How can you say that, Matt? I consented to my transformation and in doing so widowed you. I'm so, so sorry."

"It's not like you had a choice, Ali. I saw what you were going through physically—the erratic body temperature, lack of appetite and insomnia. And I felt your frustrations with the doctors' inability to diagnose you. And then to be confronted with the choice to die and end your time here on Earth, or transform into a vampire and at least have some kind of existence—all angel stuff aside—I can somewhat understand how you arrived at your decision. You were afraid to die and did what I think many in your situation would have done."

I sniffed and turned away, wiping beneath my eyes to fix my eyeliner. How could he be so understanding? And then I lost all control. My shoulders trembled in unison with my moans as tears flowed freely. I stooped to the ground and wrapped my arms around my legs, hugging myself. Matt rushed to my side.

"Ali, look at me. We'll get you through this, okay?"

"We?"

"Yes, we. I will help you with whatever you need, with whatever this is that's going on."

"What about Gabriela and the rest of the Army."

"If we're God's Army and are here to protect His greatest creation, I think that includes you. My opinion, of course. You were a mortal first, before becoming a vampire, and that should mean something."

And there it was. Matt was no longer interested in me as his wife, he viewed me as his next charity case.

"I see," I said.

Matt's phone rang. He stood as he answered it. "It's Jenna," he mouthed to me. I wanted to respond, *no kidding*. There were a bunch of mmm hmm's and ah ha's before Matt told Jenna to meet us and then disconnected the call.

"We gotta go," he said. He grabbed my arm and pulled me to my feet.

"What did Jenna say? Did she find the location?"

"She sure did."

"And?"

Matt paused. "As I suspected–Buzzard's Roost. This confirms what you and I had already thought. The locations of where Felix's clues were discovered, plotted on a map, lead us to Buzzard's Roost."

"What? The same location where Felix's body was found?" My head swirled with the possibilities of what this meant. "How did Felix know he'd die at Buzzard's Roost to be able to leave us the coordinates as a clue?"

Matt raised his brow.

"Oh my gosh. He didn't know he was going to die there. Whatever he went there for got him killed."

"That's what I'm thinking. But we need to go, Ali. Now. Vincent and Lucretia are literally right around the corner and could be here any second."

"You're right. Another angel ride?"

Matt chuckled. "It's day break, Ali. I don't think flying long distances in broad daylight would be a good way to keep the existence of angels secret from the mortals."

"Good point. Where are you parked?"

"The side street next to the cemetery."

"Hey Matt?"

"Yeah?"

I walked to him and stood toe to toe. My face was level with his chest. I lifted my head to look at him. He was already peering down at me. My eyes shifted to his neck. The vein pulsed under the flesh carrying the sweet elixir I once couldn't control myself over. But things were different now. I was no longer the crazed vampire controlled by her urges. I was fully in control. I stroked his neck with a finger, tempting myself yet displaying my restraint to Matt. His forehead glistened with a film of perspiration. His eye twitched. *He's nervous*, I thought.

"Thank you. For everything."

I reached up and pulled his head to my level. We paused, gazing into each other's eyes. My stomach flipped with anticipation. I looked at his lips before closing my eyes and pressing my mouth to his.

Chapter 17

Jenna was waiting in her car as Matt parked his truck. The three of us exited the vehicles and congregated by the rear bumpers.

"Are you two sure about this?" Jenna asked.

"Yes," Matt and I responded in unison.

"I brought a GPS device to lead us to the exact spot."

"That's not necessary," I said. "Felix left this." I removed the compass from my pocket and showed her. "We think he calibrated it to lead us to whatever it is he wants me to find."

"Good. Then we can use it to see if it confirms the spot I already located."

"What? Jenna, you went out into the field alone? What were you thinking?"

"I was thinking I had a lot of time to kill waiting for you two to get here, so I made the best use of my time."

"Did you find anything?" Matt asked.

"No, that's why I asked if you were sure about the coordinates. The spot is in the middle of nowhere." Jenna pointed out to the sea of wild grass.

"I'm positive this is it," I said. "I recently dreamt about this place."

"What did you see in your dream?" Matt asked.

"Not much. But I definitely know it was this field." I closed my eyes and recalled the most recent dream. Blue skies extended as far as the eye could see, the sun blazed and buzzards floated on air currents. I had twirled among the grass enjoying the weather. This was absolutely the place I had dreamt about.

I opened my eyes and nodded in affirmation. I sniffed the air and confirmed that unlike my dream, no unwelcome visitors were present. "Jenna, lead the way."

Jenna led with her GPS device. I followed with my eyes trained on the compass, watching as the arrow shifted as I walked. Matt parted the waist-high grass allowing us to navigate more easily. I silently cursed, wishing I had worn something more hiking-appropriate than heeled boots. We climbed up one hill and then down its other side before stopping in the valley.

"This is it," Jenna said.

"This is it?" I repeated. I turned around looking at the ground as if a clue would magically be here waiting for me.

"What does the compass say?" Matt asked.

"If I'm reading this correctly, we're standing in the correct spot."

Matt grabbed the compass and nodded, confirming we were where the compass intended to lead us. The three of us looked around trying to make sense of it all.

"Did your dream reveal anything else?"

A vision flashed through my mind of being chased by two people with guns, but I couldn't see how that had any bearing on the current situation, so I didn't mention it.

"No, Matt. My dreams don't usually give me overt clues. It's more like subtle hints and then I have to figure it out from there."

"How is the key supposed to help us here?" Matt asked.

"Key?" Jenna questioned.

I pulled the key from my pocket and filled her in on the details.

"I don't know how this fits in, but there has to be something here.

My dream and every other clue has led us to this point."

"Jenna, why don't you head in that direction," Matt directed, "and I'll look over here. Ali?"

I had heard Matt, but noise off in the distance distracted me.

"Ali, what is it?"

"Did you hear that?"

Matt turned his head attempting to hear what I was listening to. "No. What is it?"

"Not sure. You two stay here." I started walking in the direction we had come from.

"And what are you going to do?"

"Let me make heads or tails of whatever this noise is first, and if it's nothing, I'll be right back."

Matt threw his hands up, resigned to the fact I'd made up my mind. He and Jenna walked in opposite directions. I stopped and closed my eyes, allowing my hearing to expand to the cusp of hunting mode. The voices I thought I'd heard were no longer there. I heard paddles cutting through water, but that wasn't out of place given the recreational nature of the nearby park. Sneakers pounded on cement, and bicycle wheels whirred by. Maybe I was overreacting.

I diverted my attention to the ground. If I knew Felix, the coordinates would be spot on. The only question was whether or not we had interpreted all of the clues correctly. Maybe the actual location of the Buzzard's Roost was the clue and there was nothing to be found here.

I kneeled and ran my hand through the grass, disrupting a bee that flew to another wild flower. I did the same with my left hand before dropping down on all fours. I parted the grass, clawing my way over the ground. Whatever was here, it had to be buried. My head swiveled left and right, eyes combing every square inch of ground. A triangular rock flush with the ground's surface caught my attention. The dirt around it looked disturbed, as if it had been recently messed with. I scurried to the stone and dug my fingernails into the dirt. The rock loosened, allowing my fingertips underneath it in order to remove it. I jarred it free and peered into the hole. "Guys, I think I found something." Jenna and Matt jogged over to me.

"What is it?" Jenna huffed.

"Not sure yet." I shoved my hands into the hole, clawing at dirt. Several scoops later, I extracted a box. Considering how easy it was to remove from the ground, I concluded it hadn't been buried long. The metal wasn't rusted and the exterior wasn't worn, further confirming my conclusion. I rotated the box in my hands like a Rubik's Cube. There was a medium sized keyhole. An inscription encircled the hole: The Truth Will Set You Free. I sat back on my heels.

"I don't suppose this appeared in your dream?" Matt asked.

"It most definitely did not."

"I guess we know what the key is for," Jenna said.

"I guess so."

"Are you going to open it?"

"No. Not here."

"Why not?"

"Shhhh, do you hear that?" I asked.

"Hear what?"

I held up my hand to silence both of them and closed my eyes to concentrate. "Voices. Familiar voices coming from…" I stood and turned. "Coming from over there." I opened my eyes.

"That's the direction of the spillway," Jenna said, referring to the manmade damn dividing the fishing lake and swimming hole via waterfall. "Ali, it could be anyone. It could be people fishing in the lake or families swimming."

"No, no, it's just out of ear shot for me to get a good listen without using my hunting hearing. And it's further east, away from the rec area. Maybe in the marshland? But I'm telling you, I know these voices. Wait here." I placed the box in Jenna's hands. "I'll be back."

I jumped up and kicked it into full vampire gear. I arrived at a tree and without pausing, leapt onto the trunk and climbed my way up. Perching on a branch, I scoured the area. The fishing lake was calm, barely a ripple from the gentle breeze. A handful of fishing boats floated in and out of view between the treetops impeding my view. Beyond that, water spilled over into a smaller lake below. From what I could see at this angle, families had started gathering, laying out blankets and firing up grills. I closed my eyes again to key in on the voices. It took a moment but I picked up whispers to my right. The only thing in that direction was swampy marshland, but the area was off limits to park goers. Unless, of course, someone with other intentions and no regard for rules was there.

I leapt tree-to-tree circling the marsh. The voices became louder, indicating I was headed in the right direction. I settled into a pine tree and separated the branches. What I saw almost made me fall from my perch.

"What in the hell are they doing here?" I cursed.

Delilah paused as if she had heard me. I dipped the branches for camouflage. She quickly looked around before returning her attention to her companions.

Parting the branches again, I spied on the activities below. Delilah and crew stood in a clearing, marshland trimmed with cattails behind them, woods in front of them blocking the view of anyone who might be on the bridle path. Considering they didn't have horses with them, they were certainly off the beaten path. I scrambled down the tree and ran back to Matt and Jenna.

"Where'd you go?" Matt asked.

"We have a problem. Well, three to be exact."

"What's going on?"

"Delilah is here. With Caz and Jal."

"What?" Matt asked. "Why? And how is Jal out roaming freely with his partners in crime? I thought the gypsies were handling him after catching him red handed practicing magic he shouldn't have been."

"I thought so too, but it doesn't matter now. We have a bigger problem. I think Jal is up to his old tricks. I think he's going to cast a spell."

"What makes you think that?" Jenna asked.

"Well for one, he has the spell book with him. The same one he had on Rattlesnake Island when he opened the portal to the Garden. He had his hands raised in the air and was starting to chant something. His cohorts were watching his every move."

"Do you think he's trying to access the Garden again?"

"I don't know what those three are up to, but whatever it is, I'm guessing it isn't anything good. I have to stop them."

"Ali, you're not alone in this," Matt said. "We can help."

"Yeah, what do you need us to do?" Jenna asked.

I almost protested but remembered what Vincent had said, how I needed to learn to accept help and not do it all on my own. "Um, I don't know. I don't even know what I'm going to do. Maybe back me up if things get ugly?"

"We can do that," Matt said. "You go in and make them think you're alone, and we'll be there to jump in when needed."

"Okay, sounds good. I'm going to go this way," I curved my arm eastward, "and sneak up on them using the bridle path."

"We'll head west, trapping them since the marsh will prevent them from escaping."

Matt and Jenna turned to take off in the opposite direction when we all stopped.

"Well, well, well," Gabriela admonished.

I stopped dead in my tracks, inches from running into Gabriela. I peered into her chocolate brown eyes, narrowed to slits. Her arms crossed over her chest as her wings retreated into her back.

"Look what we have here," she said.

Five angels stood behind her. I looked over my shoulder and saw five others had stopped Matt and Jenna.

"What is this about?" Matt asked.

Gabriela arched an eyebrow and pursed her lips, silently indicating we should know.

"How did you find us?" Jenna asked.

"I overheard your little phone call earlier today."

"Oh God, I'm so sorry." Jenna looked at Matt and me.

"Don't give yourself too much of a hard time. With all of the vampires running around town the past few days, we knew something was going on, so the Army was on high alert. And with Matthew getting sucked into the drama, we figured it was something big."

"Avenging Felix's death is not your concern," I said.

"If that's what you're up to, then that's true. But with Matthew involved, it is my concern. You chose to ignore warning after warning and here you are again. So I'm going to ask one final time—what's going on?"

"Gabriela—" Jenna started.

"You don't get to talk," Gabriela interjected. "You ungrateful brat."

"Hey! What is your problem? I'm not an angel."

"I bring you into this flock, give you the Army's protection, save you from the vampires' wrath and how do you thank me? By sneaking behind my back and rendezvousing with Lorenzo. And then you've involved yourself in whatever these two are up to."

Jenna bit her lip and dropped her head. She kicked at a stone while she shoved her hands in her pocket, having been put in her place by Gabriela.

"Why the small army of angels, Gabriela?" Matt asked.

"They're here to help me take care of a problem." Gabriela focused her eyes on me.

"And what exactly does that mean?" I asked.

"We need to permanently take care of this." Gabriela motioned her finger between Matt and me.

"By permanent, I assume you mean you want to kill me?" I scoffed, trying to downplay the threat, but it rang loud and clear. "You can't do that."

"Oh yes I can, and I will. It would take too long to discipline Matt following Army protocol, so we'll take care of the other part of the equation."

"You can't kill me for no reason. You'd start a war!"

"Don't you think I've thought of that?" she asked. "Do you take me for an idiot?"

"There's no way you'd get away with it," I countered.

Gabriela chuckled. "Oh Allison, of course I would. It seems you have a bit of a history, one filled with lots of dead bodies and skeletons in your closet."

"You can't kill me for past murders; you can only kill me if you catch me in the act of killing a human."

"Duh," Gabriela mocked.

"You're going to frame me?"

"Is it so hard to believe? Given your past ripper ways and the fact you haven't been out of rehab too long, I don't think it's that unbelievable you fell off the wagon and we caught you red handed. And look, all the pieces are coming together. We have a human here." She smiled at Jenna.

My eyes went wide when I realized Gabriela was going to frame me for killing my best friend. Heck, it wasn't a bad plan–I had almost attacked Jenna once before. I was sure Gabriela could sell it to the Drakes and avoid a conflict.

"So that means you're going to kill me too," Matt said. "I'd be a witness to all of this and would be a liability to you."

Gabriela sneered. "I foresee many years of captivity for you because of your insubordination. If you want to live, you'll keep your mouth shut and serve out your time. If you can't keep your mouth shout, well then...."

"I've about had it with your antics," I shouted. "You want to be the judge, jury and executioner? Who do you think you are?"

I charged Gabriela. She unsheathed her sword. My skin hardened into its protective armor. As we were about to engage, Matt stepped between us. Facing Gabriela, he said, "You can't kill one of your own. That would be a death sentence for you."

"I'm not going to kill you, Matthew, now get out of my way."

"I'm not talking about me. I'm talking about Allison."

"What?" Gabriela stumbled back as if the words had physically struck her.

"What are you talking about?" I asked.

"Allison is an angel."

Gabriela scoffed. "Nice try, Matthew, but that's a pretty lame attempt to save your ex-wife."

"It's the truth."

I grabbed Matt's arm and turned him toward me. He looked me in the eye and nodded.

"How?" I asked.

"Yes, enlighten us about this new revelation," Gabriela demanded.

Matt turned to her. "You see, Gabriela, there is more going on here than meets the eye. After Felix's murder, Ali got a posthumous note from Felix stating he discovered how and why Ali was the first descendant to exhibit signs of vampirism."

Gabriela rolled her eyes.

"The note said there was a clue in Ali's family tree, so Jenna and I did a little research and found something. I noticed an anomaly in the recording of some surnames about a thousand years ago, and when I cross referenced it with the Army's files, I discovered someone tried to conceal the fact that an angel had married a descendant many moons ago."

"Although I find that impossible, if it's true, it still doesn't require your intervention."

"Ah, but it does," Matt responded. "When wooden bullets from our arsenal were used to kill Felix."

"What are you talking about? We don't have any such weapons."

Matt threw her a look that said try again.

All emotion drained from Gabriela's face. "How do you know about those bullets? That information is privy to the senior most members of the Army."

Matt threw me a look.

"I borrowed your access pass and did a little sleuthing." Gabriela attempted to respond but Matt cut her off. "Don't deny it. I saw the case with my own eyes and saw that there were missing bullets. Ali has a scar proving the bullets were used. Ali, show her your hand."

I held up my thumb so Gabriela could see the brand left by the bullet.

"Why didn't you say something sooner, Matthew?"

"Like I knew who I could trust in the Army? You said it yourself, those weapons are secure. And someone with security clearance such as yourself, well I didn't know…."

"Are you accusing me of killing Felix?"

"Guys," I interrupted. "This is all good stuff, but we have a more pressing need at the moment." I nudged my head in the direction of the marsh.

"What's going on?" Gabriela asked.

"Rattlesnake Island part two," I responded.

"Come again?"

Flashes of light fractured the sky. It sounded like an M-80 had gone off as the thunderous sound threw us all to the ground. Red, yellow, green and violet beams of light flickered like an electrical current. As quickly as it had appeared, everything returned to normal, except for the screams from the frantic park goers.

"What was that?" Gabriela asked.

I didn't bother responding, partly because I didn't know how to explain it. Everyone would find out soon enough.

Chapter 18

"How is this possible?" I whispered as my brain tried to comprehend what I was seeing. Moments later, Matt, Jenna, Gabriela and her crew caught up to me.

"Is that who I think it is?" Matt asked.

Jal and Caz high fived each other, too consumed in their celebration to notice we had crashed the party. Delilah ran to the fourth person who I hadn't seen earlier.

"Lucious?" I questioned.

Jal and Caz turned toward me and composed themselves. Delilah stooped down to comfort Lucious who looked like he had seen better days. He was emaciated, his cheeks hollow, and what was left of his clothing hung off him like he was a hanger. He could have used a shower too; his skin was smudged with dirt and he had a split lip and black eye.

Lucious winced as he struggled to prop himself on his elbows. When he heard me call his name, it looked as if it took every bit of what energy he had to snarl. Delilah's eyes instantly focused on me with such anger that I flinched. She snickered.

"But how?" I questioned. "You were trapped in the Garden."

"By opening a portal between both worlds," a female responded.

Everyone turned their heads and looked to the right.

"Who in the hell is she?" Delilah cursed.

"Lucretia," I responded.

Delilah scrunched her face, apparently not happy with all of the uninvited visitors. Lucious whimpered as he hoisted himself to a seated position.

"How do you know about the portal?" Caz demanded.

"Because I've been following all of you fools around for months trying to piece together what's been going on. It has been quite comical being the outsider looking in on this circus." Lucretia panned the crowd.

"You mean you've been nosing around trying to figure out why Vincent left you for me," I challenged, defiance in my voice. Someone grabbed my arm. It was Jenna, with a look on her face as if asking what the heck I was doing.

Lucretia scoffed. "There's more going on here than meets the eye, Allison. There are bigger things brewing. These three clowns," she pointed to Jal, Caz and Delilah, "have been so consumed with finding a way to free Lucious that they got sloppy and didn't notice me tailing them."

"Why would they? Why would they have had any inclination they were being followed?"

"Ha, you're right." Lucretia walked to Jal and placed a finger under his chin, momentarily looking into his eyes before feigning boredom and walking past him. "Maybe the better question is why would I have thought to have followed them, hmm? Wouldn't you all like to know?" She turned and faced me.

"That is an excellent question," Vincent called out from the tree line.

"Now the gang's all here," Matt quipped under his breath.

"I for one would like to know," Vincent said as he marched toward the action.

Lucretia's mouth curled into a grin. With her blood red lips, black eye shadow and pale skin, she resembled the Joker. "Ah, Vincent. So nice of you to join us." She didn't sound the least bit surprised to see him. "It's all quite simple actually. All I had to do was open my eyes and observe." Lucretia turned and looked at everyone. "No? None of you know what I'm talking about? Last year's Halloween party at the Drake's castle. You all seem to forget I was there. I saw these three," she twirled her finger in the direction of Caz, Lucious and Delilah, "show up and I saw how much their unexpected visit bothered you, Vincent." She stopped in front of Vincent, a permanent snicker plastered on her face. Vincent stared back, expressionless. "From one of the castle windows, I watched your little exchange taking place. Although I couldn't hear over that horrendous music, I could tell by your gestures you weren't pleased. And then your little girlfriend over there piqued Delilah's interest when she opened the second story window, the breeze carrying her scent down to all of you. Delilah straightened like a soldier called to attention. And then there was Lucious' reaction to Allison's presence. He went toe-to-toe with you like you were two hungry dogs fighting for the last piece of meat. Oh, I knew something was up. You all wouldn't react like that to just any mortal. So I started following them."

Vincent's lip quivered.

"Did I touch a nerve?"

Lucretia strutted over to me. Matt extended his sword between her and me. Lucretia rolled her eyes. "Oh please," she said.

I touched Matt's wrist and looked at him. I nodded, indicating it would be okay. At least that's what I felt at the moment. I didn't think Lucretia would cause me harm with so many around.

"Aren't you the least bit curious?" she asked me as she flipped her knee-length hair over her shoulder.

I was curious about a lot of things at the moment but didn't know what she was specifically referring to, so I said nothing.

"Hmm? You got nothing?"

Looking beyond her, I said, "I am curious how Jal is here considering he was supposed to be punished by the gypsy elders for practicing magic last March."

Lucretia burst out in laughter, but she was the only one. She calmed herself and said, "Oh, the gypsy elders punished him all right. He was incarcerated, but those two," she pointed to Caz and Delilah, "broke him out because they needed his skill set."

Caz nodded his head as if proud of the achievement. Delilah slugged him in the ribs. He jumped aside, rubbing where he'd been struck, and then composed himself.

"Apparently they needed his magical abilities to open a portal and free Lucious."

"Exactly. But doesn't any of this seem suspicious to you?" Lucretia waved her hand around a la Vanna White.

My eyes darted to the sound of rustling coming from behind Vincent. The Drakes appeared. How on Earth had they found us? Then, the image of the man at the bus stop popped into my mind. He must have been the vampire Max had ordered to follow me when I accessed the hunting app, and he must have had him follow me this morning as well.

"Hello brothers, sister," Vincent inclined his head toward them, looking less than pleased they had joined.

All three looked stunned at the scene they had happened upon.

"What have we missed?" Lorenzo asked.

"We were just getting to the good part," Lucretia said, rubbing her hands together. She turned and faced me. "Well? Anything?"

I threw up my arms in frustration. "I don't know. There's Jal, his spell book, we're surrounded by nature which is what he needs to do his magic."

"Ah ha!" She rose up on her toes and pointed her index finger at me. "Come on, Allison. You were there in March, I wasn't. Following these guys around, I learned that Jal needs a significant amount of nature–water, sky, land–in order to pull off the type of magic needed to open the portal. Does this look like that type of place to you?"

My eyes flitted around the surroundings. The marsh was considerably different from Rattlesnake Island which was surrounded by Lake Erie. There was less water here and limited access to it, and the canopy impeded access to the sky. "Well, I guess not."

"Your guess is correct. So if he couldn't pool nature's power, how do you think he compensated?"

"Lucretia–" Vincent started.

"No, no, no. You're not going to stop me now. Think about it, Allison. What could a gypsy use as part of his spell that would be so powerful it could open a portal big enough for this one," she pointed to Lucious, "to escape through?"

"You obviously know the answer, so why don't you enlighten us."

Lucretia smiled, folding her hands and raising them to her mouth as she paced. She strummed her fingers like a mad scientist. "A blood more potent and pure than Cain's."

"What?" I gasped. Matt, Jenna and the angels broke out in chatter.

"You don't know what you're talking about," Vincent challenged. His brothers held him back from charging.

"Seems I've touched a nerve again."

"But how…" My mind blanked. So Lucretia knew I was a descendant and hadn't said anything until now? But why? Why would she have kept this a secret? Why wouldn't she have confronted me sooner or told the Ruling Council?

Lucretia flexed her jaw and sighed. "You seem to forget I dated Vincent for centuries. I knew he was a historian. I knew I'd find answers in his historical accounts, although I didn't think it would be as hard as it was since the records I needed weren't at Castle Adena. And once I thought to search your house, there it was, all laid out for me in your den, Allison. You're a descendant of Cain." She walked over to Vincent who was still restrained by his brothers. His chest heaved and his face reddened. "That's quite the secret you managed to hold onto all of these years, Secret Coven," she hissed as she calculatingly looked at each Drake.

"This is all a good story," Lucious stated. He was standing, propped up by Delilah and Caz, "but this isn't new news. We knew Allison was a descendant when we met her. There's no mistaking the scent she carries. All descendants smell like the Garden of Eden."

Another laugh. "Ah, I see Vincent hasn't told you the whole story."

"Lucretia," Vincent shouted. "Don't you dare!"

"Or what? What are you going to do to me when I tell these guys that Cain fathered a child with a mortal after he was transformed into a vampire?"

"What?" Lucious gasped. Delilah, Caz and Jal looked confusedly at each other as they mumbled questions about vampires procreating with humans.

"You mean to tell me," Lucious shouted, "there are mortals running around out there with the Devil's venom in their blood?"

"That's exactly what I'm saying," Lucretia said.

I dropped my head. Now that Lucious and his cronies knew there were more descendants, I could only imagine what was running through their minds. If my blood could unlock the portal to the Garden of Eden, what could the blood of multiple descendants unlock? I could see their minds turning over with the possibilities.

"Don't get any ideas," Gabriela warned. "Saint Michael's Army will fiercely defend the lives of descendants as we do any other mortal. Their soul is as precious as any."

"So what happened then?" Caz asked as he flipped a hand in my direction, insinuating the Army had failed to protect me.

"Why you..." Gabriela launched into flight as two of her soldiers grabbed her legs, reeling her in.

"I knew there had to be a reason why Allison's blood worked to counter the spell concealing the Garden when the blood from other descendants didn't," Jal surmised.

"So, what? You saved some of my blood from this past March and used it for the spell today?"

"Are you seriously that dense?" Lucretia questioned. "Your loving Vincent," she looked at me and pointed at him, "has been using you."

"What do you mean?"

"Allison," Vincent called out, "don't believe anything she says."

My eyes darted between him and Lucretia. Which one could I trust?

"I have your attention now, don't I?" Lucretia asked. She turned and shouted to Vincent. "Perhaps you'd like to tell her?"

Vincent clamped his mouth shut and twisted his head as if threatening Lucretia to not to say a word. Lucretia looked back at me and arched her brows waiting for me to say something. I looked over my shoulder at Matt and Jenna, and then at Gabriela and the other angels. The box in Jenna's hands caught my attention. I grabbed it from her.

"I don't trust any of you." I held the box in my left hand and shook it in the air.

"What's that?" Vincent eyed the box with curiosity.

"This?" I shook the box again and then pulled it to my chest. "This is the truth. Straight from Felix."

"Allison, what are you talking about?" Marlo asked.

"A few days after Felix's death, I received a letter from him.""A letter from Felix after he died? But how?" Marlo asked.

"It was sent via courier. The note said that if I received the letter, then something bad had come of him." I looked around gauging everyone's reaction. I had piqued the Drakes' interest; in fact, it appeared I'd piqued everyone's interest. All eyes focused on me and I felt anxiety in the air with what I was about to say next.

"What else did this letter say?" Lorenzo asked.

I cleared my throat. "It said that Felix had been researching me to figure out how I was so strong for a vampire so young."

Vincent shifted his weight. "That's no surprise. We all knew he was doing that."

"What's with the attitude?" Marlo questioned.

"Nothing," Vincent responded defensively. "I mean we've all known about the existence of descendants for centuries. What happened to Allison was bound to happen to a descendant at some point and Felix would have wanted to research. That stuff intrigued him."

I interjected. "The note also said the truth would find me. And after receiving the letter, I received a series of clues that led me to this." I held up the container.

Vincent's eyes narrowed.

"What is that?" Max asked as he walked toward me.

A husky angel stepped in his path. "You can hold it right about there," the angel said.

Max sized up the man. "Really? What do you think I'm going to do here?"

"It's okay," I called out. "Although Felix's letter said to trust no one, not even his siblings, I don't think Max will do anything. Not with all of these people here."

Max cocked his head. "Felix said that?"

I nodded. "This," I held up the box, "I suppose is the truth Felix wanted me to find." I turned the box over, locating the keyhole. I reached into my back pocket and pulled out the skeleton key I'd found at Felix's cottage and inserted into the hole. The locking mechanism clicked as I turned the key. I lifted the lid and looked inside. There was a glass orb, clear with a pearlescent finish, nestled in strips of shredded paper. I pulled the globe out of the box and held it at eye level. I rotated it but didn't notice any etchings or anything revealing any truth to me. "Anyone have any idea what this is?"

"Yeah," Max replied. "It's one of Felix's favorite inventions. You smash it and it releases a video message."

I scoffed. "You expect me to smash this? Felix said to not trust any of you. How do I know you're not lying?"

"He's not," Lorenzo said. "I've seen it before. We all have. Felix had toyed with the idea for decades until perfecting it a few years ago."

I looked at Marlo who nodded her head in agreement with her two brothers. I then looked at Vincent.

"Oh come on, Allison," Vincent pleaded. "Do you believe any of this? How do you know this isn't some sort of trap? If you break the globe, maybe some sort of poisonous gas will be released and kill us all. Felix said to trust no one; why would you trust a posthumous note that supposedly came from him?"

"Sounds like someone has something to hide," Gabriela murmured.

"I have nothing to hide," Vincent responded defensively. "I've only ever wanted to help Allison. I love her."

"I trust Felix," I said. "You all don't realize how much he and I interacted after my detox. I knew I was a mystery to him and he wanted to solve why I was the first descendant to exhibit signs of vampirism. I answered questions for him the best I could, but I too wanted to know once and for all, why me? So if you have nothing to hide, Vincent, you won't mind this." Clutching the globe, I raised my hand in the air and chucked the orb to the ground.

Vincent screamed and ran toward the globe. At first, I thought he was going to try to catch it, but then realized he was running toward Lucious and company who were attempting to flee. Vincent tackled them and started speaking in a foreign language, one I didn't recognize.

Lorenzo tuned a curious ear. "Brother?"

Vincent looked up and frowned. He grabbed Lucious and Delilah by the shoulders and turned them around.

Splintered glass scattered across the dirt. We all stared waiting for something to happen and when nothing did, I turned around, crossed my arms and pinched the bridge of my nose. I squeezed my eyes shut, cursing to myself about what I'd done. Had I destroyed the one clue Felix had left me that was finally going to answer all of my questions?

"Ali," Matt said. "Turn around."

I raised my head and looked at Matt. He nudged his head, motioning for me to turn, so I did.

Smoke wafted from the broken glass. White swirls snaked upward and hovered about five feet off the ground. The smoke circulated clockwise, picking up speed and forming a semi-transparent white oval. Colored streaks cracked across the surface, like a TV without frequency. The colors quickly formed a picture of Felix. Then he spoke.

"Allison, if you're seeing this, then regrettably I'm most likely no longer with you. But for you to be seeing this message means you must have received my clues and successfully solved my puzzle. I'm sorry for all of the smoke and mirrors, but it was necessary to ensure this message didn't fall into the wrong hands.

"You know that ever since your transformation, you've been a mystery to me and one I was determined to solve. Your strength alone was curious,

as no other vampire known to us has had your physical strength at such a young age. It shouldn't have been possible for you to nearly defeat Lucious, a vampire over two hundred centuries old."

Lucious' lip quivered at the mention of our battle. I smiled. *Yeah*, I thought. *I kicked his ass.*

"Then there was your insatiable appetite for human blood. Yes, newborn vampires need to feed often and be trained to control their urges, but even those who had attempted vampire life on their own without such training never had an appetite as voracious as yours.

"I know you are aware I was researching your family tree. This was a logical starting point considering you were a descendant of a vampire Cain and a mortal. We knew the Devil's venom was passed down through your mother's side, so I traced back each descendant from there, checking and double checking the records my siblings and I had maintained. And there I discovered you are not only Cain's descendant, but you're also descendent from angels."

A collective gasp escaped from the Drakes and Lucious and his crew, from everyone except Vincent who concentrated so hard on the ground as if trying to dig himself a hole to escape. Without moving his head, he shifted his eyes to me. I narrowed mine, studying his face. He looked away.

"It's true, Allison. You and Matthew aren't the first angel/vampire marriage."

I looked over at Gabriela and gave her a look as if to say, oh really.

"I recognized surnames in your tree, far back, going over a thousand years ago. So I hacked into Saint Michael's Army's databases to conduct further research."

Gabriela tightened the grip on her sword.

"You see, the Army keeps familial records on all of their archangels. I did some cross-referencing and confirmed you are descendent from angels. However, someone at some point doctored the Secret Coven's records and concealed these surnames. Why? Well, I wasn't sure. And although this was an interesting fact, it didn't answer any questions we had about your strength or appetite.

"So I continued digging, this time on your father's side. I wasn't sure what I was looking for, but given the discrepancy on your mother's side, I paid particular attention to all surnames. And sure enough, I found another discrepancy, but one that couldn't be answered by searching the Army's database. So I again turned to our historical records, the ones recorded by Vincent and stored at my family's castle."

I glared at Vincent but the coward wouldn't look at me. He was most definitely hiding something, I concluded.

"I noticed a typo in the surnames in the records I was looking at compared to the names recorded in Vincent's historical accounts. After more research, I discovered something quite interesting. Allison, your father is also a descendant."

"What?" I gasped.

Felix continued.

"I traced his lineage and discovered that he comes from a long line of descendants, offspring from Cain's affair with a mortal. This means you're the first known offspring of two descendants.

"Although I found the discovery enlightening, I wondered how this could have happened. My siblings and I had kept meticulous records of all descendants and not once did this ever pop up on our radar. So I did some more digging, digging in Secret Coven records. My siblings and I were the ones who had watched over your kind since the beginning of your bloodline and I knew the answer had to be in our records.

"I noticed a trend. There was one particular Drake sibling who seemed to be watching you during your major life events. I then looked back at your parents and noticed that this sibling also watched over them during their major life events. The pattern continued all the way back to where I found the discrepancy in surnames. Someone had intentionally changed one of your ancestor's surnames to cover up the fact that he had a hand in ultimately uniting two descendants. You see, your father's ancestors' surname was changed long ago to disguise his descendant bloodline.

"What does it all mean? Since you're descendent from two descendants, you carry double the amount of the Devil's venom in your blood, more than any other vampire or descendant. A vampire's strength comes from its venom and since you have twice as much in your system, well that explains your strength at your age. It also accounts for your voracious appetite. You simply need more blood to keep your venom satiated.

"But it also means your blood is more potent and pure than Cain's. We already knew that, but whereas we originally thought that was the case since you were a descendant transformed into a vampire, I now know it's the case because of your parents' bloodlines. No ordinary descendant's blood was going to unlock the Garden of Eden. I assume Lucious and Jal had previously attempted that without success. Knowing the counter spell existed, *and knowing they needed extremely rare blood, there was one person they knew they could go to, someone who had an affinity for rare and unique things—Vincent.*

"Allison, I believe Vincent orchestrated the whole thing. He was primarily responsible for maintaining descendant records and was the one watching over your family's major life events. I believe he was the one who changed the surname to conceal your father's bloodline and it was Vincent who had a hand in your parent's marriage. I believe he hoped their union would produce offspring, a child whose blood could unlock the Garden. It makes sense. We all know about Vincent's penchant for rare and unique items. Why wouldn't access to the Garden be on his wish list of things to own? Vincent has lied to you from the beginning. He lied to my siblings, and to me, too.

"But I have lied too and have a confession to make. The video that was played for the Ruling Council proving you consented to your transformation, it was doctored. Allison, I'm sorry. Vincent asked me to alter the evidence in order to spare his life. When I first said no, he threatened me. He said he'd kill my brother. No, not one of the Drake siblings but my blood brother, Ezekiel. Beyond that, he threatened to expose me from having transformed Zeke without his permission and that truth would have resulted in my death."

As if on cue, smoke wafted above the ground in the space between the Drakes and Lucious. The vapors floated upward and inward forming the shape of a person and then a man came into view. He had brown hair with golden highlights that flowed past his shoulders, brown eyes with thirteen gold flecks and Felix's nose – this was the butler from Castle Adena who had escorted me upstairs to wait for the Drakes when I arrived at the castle upon first hearing of Felix's death. This was also the man who had appeared at Riverside Cemetery and had given me the

Ulee note. This was Felix's brother. This was Zeke.

Felix continued.

"It's true. I committed that crime thousands of years ago out of fear. I didn't want to go through this life on my own. Those were the early days of this coven and things were much different. We didn't feel like a family then. I needed companionship, so I selfishly transformed Zeke. He's stayed away all of these years to hide my dirty little secret. Although Zeke eventually came to terms with what I had done to him, he didn't want to see me die, punished for this crime. When Vincent threatened me, I cowered and caved. I consented to helping him. I'm so sorry, Allison, and I hope you can forgive me."

Tears slid down Felix's cheeks. He attempted to brush them away with his hands, but not soon enough before temporary scars marred his complexion.

"The closer I got to uncovering the truth about you, the more I felt someone or something following me. It was as if death loomed around every corner the closer I got to the truth. But for as much as I could sense someone was following me, I could never catch that person. Allison, a skilled huntsman was shadowing my every move, I think waiting to see what I was going to discover or if I was going to unearth the truth. That is why I warned you in my first clue not to trust anyone, not even my siblings. I didn't know if Vincent was following me, or one of my other siblings, or Caz or Delilah or someone else. Lord knows I've made enough enemies over the centuries.

"I've made peace with all of it, Allison. If it's my time to die, I am ready for it. I've done a lot of damage over the centuries and have damned so many innocent human souls in order to survive. I've asked God for

forgiveness, that when I die, He grant me reprieve and spare me from an afterlife toiling in Hell. But if suffering in Hell is what I must do for penance, then so be it. There's still hope that I've lived my life in such a way that God will realize at the End of Days I attempted to limit the damage I've inflicted in the name of the Devil just so I could live forever.

"But just because I'm dead doesn't mean I don't want to see my killer brought to justice. I challenge you with this. When you find the person or persons responsible, don't kill them. We don't need to punish one death with another. That's the easy way out. Death will end their suffering too easily. Lock them up and throw away the key. Let them rot in a jail cell for eternity, with plenty of time to think about what they've done. Starve them of blood, let them suffer as their skin hardens into a tomb and their mind will have nothing else to do but think about what got them into this situation. That is punishment death will negate. That is true punishment.

"Allison, I hope this truth brings you peace. Until we meet again, your brother, Felix."

The video flickered and then with a flash of light, was gone.

Silence filled the immediate area. My head bowed, I sucked in a breath realizing I hadn't breathed throughout the duration of the video. Matt placed a hand on my shoulder and I shook him off. Jenna called out my name but I raised a hand to silence her. I needed to process what I had just heard.

Marlo started yelling first. I shifted my eyes without raising my head and saw her charging across the space toward Vincent. Her brothers followed. Vincent stood with arms crossed, feet firmly planted. Lucious leered and Delilah and Caz looked on with a curious eye. Jal slinked behind them. The angels charged from behind me to join the melee. I was frozen in place.

My mother and my father were both descendants. The Devil's blood had run through both of them. I was descendent from angels as well. My parents married because of Vincent's tampering. I was a result of that marriage. I was a result of Vincent's meddling. I was a vampire today because Vincent orchestrated my parent's marriage hoping offspring would be produced, the blood of which would be the key to unlocking the Garden. Matt and I were no longer together because of Vincent's actions.

I shifted my gaze to Vincent. He and Marlo shouted at each other, fingers pointing, spit flying. Tears brimmed in my eyes. They weren't tears of pity for my situation, they were tears of rage. My entire life had been one big manipulation. The angels had sent Matt into my life with the unintended consequence of us marrying. That wasn't supposed to have happened but it did. We weren't supposed to have happened. But we did. The angels had ruined Matt's life as much as Vincent had ruined mine.

I palmed my temples, fingers fisting my hair. I pulled, hoping the physical pain would alleviate the mental anguish, but it didn't. Matt put a hand on my back. I stared at the ground, unable to hear him as my mind was consumed with what we all had learned. Jenna's feet came into view and I heard her murmurs. I blinked, tears rolled. My body numbed. I glanced at the crowd. They looked like a bunch of school kids in a playground argument. I dropped to my knees, hunching over, burying my head between my knees, hands folded over my neck. Matt and Jenna bent down, both asking if I was okay.

I straightened and looked at both of them through tear-blurred vision. Their eyes were wide with concern, foreheads wrinkled, as they waited for me to say something.

"Stop!" I yelled. I rose up on my knees. The crowd turned and looked at me. "Just stop."

My chest heaved with every breath, palms sweating. The numbness faded, replaced with a tingly sensation–venom mixed with adrenaline.

Angels restrained Vincent, Caz, Delilah, Lucious and Jal. I placed my left foot on the ground, lifted myself, then planted the right foot. My gaze locked on Vincent like a missile to a target. I seethed about how infuriatingly handsome he was, those looks a deception that had blinded me for so long. I loathed the man. At least the impassioned emotion helped further bury the effects of the creator's bond. No more would I feel any emotion other than contempt for him. I took off running, Matt and Jenna failing to stop me. As I approached Vincent, Lorenzo stepped into my path, scooping me up with one arm around my chest and under my arms. I kicked at the air, tears stinging my skin. Lorenzo placed me on my feet.

"How dare you," I shouted and pointed at Vincent. "You are not God. You can't manipulate people's lives, but that's exactly what you've done and what's worse is you've done it for your own gain. How many lives have you altered, huh? How many? Mine, Matt's, my parents, grandparents, how many others? All in an effort to change fate and reap the benefits. And then you lie to my face about my transformation multiple times. You son of a bitch! How could you?"

Vincent stared at me, his features soft. He wasn't angry, he was calm. And that infuriated me even more. "You may not have consented, Allison, but that doesn't change the way I feel about you. I love you."

"Bullshit," I spat. "You don't love me. You don't know what it means to love. You used Lucretia and her abilities as a seer to amass riches, you used Felix and his technical abilities to save your life, and you used me to gain access to the Garden of Eden. You don't do those sorts of things to people you love."

"I asked Felix to alter the video of your transformation so we could be together forever."

"Are you delusional? You blackmailed Felix into doctoring the video to cover your own ass. But I'm sure in your warped, little mind you had hoped we'd ride off into the sunset together. And you almost got your wish."

I turned and paced to blow off steam before I used Vincent as a punching bag.

"How long have you been working with these guys?" Lorenzo asked, waving a hand between Lucious and his cronies.

Vincent didn't respond. I turned. Vincent had a cocky smirk on his face. Lucious stared straight ahead at the ground. Caz looked up at the sky, Delilah looked off into the woods and Jal hid behind Caz.

"What was in it for you, Vincent?" I asked. "Were you all supposed to go through the portal together and live happily ever after in the Garden?"

"Oh he's been working with them all right," Lucretia said. "Tell her how you helped them access the portal today in order to free Lucious.

Vincent sneered. "You know nothing."

"Oh darling," Lucretia replied. "Tailing you was so easy. You tell her, or I will."

Vincent licked his lips while staring down Lucretia, almost as if daring her to say something.

Lucretia huffed. "Allison, have you felt exceptionally weak lately? Even after feeding, have you not felt like yourself?"

"Yes," I replied tentatively, unsure where this was going. My thoughts traveled back to my most recent episode at the cemetery when I felt drained after my long run to get there. I had spent the previous night with Vincent.

"Lucretia," Vincent called out.

Lucretia smiled. "That's because Vincent, here, has been siphoning your blood to give to these fools," she pointed at Caz and Delilah, "to help Delilah spring her man from an eternity in the Garden."

"What?" I hissed. My hand instinctively touched my neck where Vincent had previously bitten me. I felt violated. Our most intimate moments were nothing more than a sham, easy access to my blood. "I suppose this explains why Caz and Delilah showed up at Felix's funeral, doesn't it? They were there to pressure you, Vincent, right? To hurry you along and give them my blood so they could save their beloved Lucious. Am I right?"

"Can you blame me?" Delilah cried out. "I couldn't leave my lover in there with Cain. I feared for his life."

"Cain is alive?" Lucretia questioned and glanced at everyone.

"Mmm hmm," Marlo responded.

Lucretia opened her mouth, but Marlo indicated she'd fill her in later.

"How in the world was there a portal available to be opened and allow this to happen?" Marlo asked.

"It was a fail safe," Gabriela responded, "implemented for Cain's benefit if there were ever a need to extract him from the Garden without having to go through the full ritual like you witnessed on Rattlesnake Island. Fewer natural resources are needed, but to compensate, more blood is required for the spell to work."

"And you obliged?" I asked Vincent. "How could you? How could you do that to me?"

Vincent was silent.

"Answer me, damn it."

"They threatened your safety."

"Oh come on. You don't have anything better than that? Caz and Delilah already knew my blood was the key. It's not like they were going to kill me."

"They knew your blood was key, but they didn't know why... until now. They had no idea both of your parents were descendants and that was the reason your blood was more potent and pure than Cain's. They wouldn't have killed you, but if I didn't help them, they would have captured and tortured you. And believe it or not, Allison, I love you and was trying to protect you."

"The only person you love is yourself. What about Felix? You killed him, didn't you?"

"No," Vincent roared as he strained against the angels who were restraining him. "I may be a lot of things, but I'm not a killer. I did not kill my brother."

Zeke walked to the center of the circle.

"Sure you did," Zeke said. "You were aware my brother was researching Allison's lineage, looking for answers. He got too close to exposing you for who you really are and you killed him."

"I did not kill Felix," Vincent said, calm and steady. He took three deep breaths. "They did." Without looking, Vincent pointed behind him at Caz and Delilah. They both shifted uncomfortably. "They were growing impatient with how long it was taking me to obtain Allison's blood. They threatened that they were willing to show me how serious they were. I thought it meant harming Allison, but I guess they found another way."

"You expect us to believe Caz and Delilah killed Felix?" Matt questioned. "How could they? How would they have had access to wooden bullets made from the wood of the cross Jesus was crucified on?"

"What?" one of the angels gasped. Gabriela dropped her head, the secret officially out.

The Drakes looked around at each other.

"It's true," Matt confirmed. He grabbed my hand and held it up for the angels to see. "Ali touched one of the bullets that killed Felix and was branded with the seal of Saint Michael's Army which is engraved in the bullets."

"I have the same scar," Max said and held up his hands.

"I can also confirm six bullets are missing from the Army's arsenal," Matt said.

Gabriela threw him a look.

"How would Caz and Delilah have gotten the bullets?" Marlo asked.

"How would I know?" Vincent responded. "How would I have gotten to the bullets if you think I killed our brother? It's not like I have easy access to a member of the flock." Vincent glared at Lorenzo.

"Oh come on, brother," Lorenzo said, "you're grasping at straws. You think because of my relationship with Jenna I somehow obtained the bullets?"

"The thought crossed my mind."

"What motive would I possibly have to do something like that? If the bullets belong to the Army, then isn't there only one answer as to who used the bullets and murdered our brother?"

"Are you accusing the Army of killing Felix?" Gabriela questioned. "We're not that dumb, Lorenzo. We wouldn't kill a vampire for no reason and risk the certainty of starting a war."

"Well the bullets somehow made it out of the cache and were used to kill Felix," Matt said.

"What about her?" Marlo asked and nodded her head toward Jenna.

"Me?" Jenna exclaimed. "You have to be kidding me. I've barely left Matt's house since the incident in March, fearful of running into someone who might kill me."

"You live with two archangels which gives you easy access to what they know."

"But I didn't kill Felix," Jenna pleaded. "I mean even if I had the bullets, how would I have snuck up on a vampire to kill him?"

"She raises a valid point," I said.

Delilah chuckled and Caz reprimanded her.

I turned toward Delilah. "What's so funny?"

"Nothing." She shrugged her shoulders, feigning ignorance.

My eyes darted between Caz and Delilah, studying their expressions. Neither would return my stare. They were hiding something. "You two killed Felix, didn't you?"

"Us?" Caz exclaimed. "But how could we? We certainly didn't have access to the bullets."

"I don't know how, but it was you. I saw you both in my dreams. You were chasing me through the Buzzard's Roost field, as I assume you chased Felix down. When I stopped running in my dream, I saw two figures pointing guns at me."

"You're going to charge us with murder based on a dream?"

"Allison's dreams are more than that," Marlo responded. "They're more like coded messages that need to be deciphered and it seems we've solved her latest dream."

"But she only saw figures," Delilah exclaimed. "They could have been anyone."

"What two other people do we know had motive to harm someone close to Vincent?" I asked.

"But how would they have known such bullets existed?" Max asked. "We certainly hadn't heard of them before."

"That's what happens when you have contacts on the street," Vincent mumbled.

"Or moles in the Army," Lorenzo countered.

"How dare you–" Gabriela started.

"Gabriela," Matt said. "Don't. Others within the Army ranks have heard rumors about these bullets."

"What?"

"I recently heard the rumors at the last Army meeting. There must be a mole in the Army; someone willing to sell this weapon for a price, and they obviously found a buyer."

Gabriella was about to protest when she was cut off.

"There's plenty of time to review your personnel issues later," Lucretia said. "We need to wrap this up before we attract unwanted attention." She was referring to the chaos that had ensued after the sudden burst of lightning and thunder causing the park's visitors to flee.

"I say we honor Felix's wishes and jail the lot of them," I offered.

Lucretia smirked. "Are you a seated member of the Council?" I shook my head. "I didn't think so. What happens to them isn't up to you."

"As a seated member of the Council, I think it's worthy of consideration," Lorenzo said. "Vincent has tampered with our historical accounts, documents we've used, that the Ruling Council has used, to make strategic decisions over the past 2,000 years. There's no telling what damage we may have unknowingly done based on inaccurate information. If we kill him, we lose all hope of correcting our records and righting our wrongs."

"You know that's a call we can't make ourselves," Lucretia reminded.

"I know. We need to take this, all of this, to the Council."

"Agreed."

"And what about the rest of them?" Lucretia pointed at Lucious and his gang.

"We take them to the Council as well and try them for their crimes."

"Hello," Lucious quipped. "You seem to forget we don't belong to your little sect of vampire society. Your rules don't apply to us."

Lucretia scoffed. "Given what has transpired here today and what I've learned over the past months, I think the Council will be quite interested in what you've been up to and the havoc you've wreaked."

"And as for you," Lorenzo pointed at Jal. "If your kind couldn't keep you incarcerated for your crimes, we'll be happy to offer you a cell in our prison."

"The elders of my tribe will never go for it."

"We'll see about that."

Someone cleared his or her throat. Zeke appeared from behind the crowd.

"If you don't mind, may I attend the Council meeting?"

"Of course," Lorenzo responded. "Felix was your brother. You should be there to hear what justice is handed out. Isn't that right, Lucretia?"

Lucretia narrowed her eyes. "Only seated members and members of their coven are permitted at the meetings."

"Then consider Zeke part of our coven."

Zeke nodded his head in acceptance. "Thank you." He turned to me. "Allison, I'm sorry for being so enigmatic over the past few days. After Felix died, I too received a letter. He asked for my help to ensure you discovered the truth. He also told me not to trust anyone and is the reason I didn't reveal my true identity to you. I hope you can forgive me for starting our relationship off on false pretenses."

"Zeke, there's no need to apologize. Thank you for everything you've done to help me get to this point. Say, was that you who scrawled the message on my back door yesterday morning?"

He blushed as much as a vampire could. "It was. Felix had requested I deliver that clue to you, in addition to the Ulee note, and to ensure you discovered his magical painting."

I smiled and Zeke returned the gesture. "I'm so sorry for your loss."

"Thank you. I appreciate the sentiment." We embraced.

"Do you need assistance transporting the prisoners?" Gabriela asked.

"Thanks for offering," Lucretia said. "I'll take you up on that. We could use an extra hand."

The angels shoved the prisoners toward the bridle path, Lucretia leading the way, but Gabriela remained behind.

"Thank you for your help today," Lorenzo said to her.

She half smiled. "There's still one more matter to be addressed."

"And what would that be?"

Gabriela shifted her eyes to Matt and me.

"What's there to discuss?"

"Yeah, Gabriela, what is there to discuss?" Matt asked. "You heard earlier that Ali is part angel."

My heart fluttered. Matt was defending me!

"And she's also a vampire. And you are a member of Saint Michael's Army."

"Let me guess what you're going to say. We can't be together, right?"

"That's right," Gabriela stated defiantly, chin held high.

"I'm tired of hearing it, Gabriela."

"Watch your tone of voice. I'm your superior."

"Not any more. I quit the Army."

"You can't quit the Army. You were born an angel and are now fully knighted. This isn't something you can just walk away from."

"Watch me. There's no longer any reason why Ali and I can't be together. She's part angel; that negates all of your rules. I'm walking away from my Army duties and walking away with Ali, if she'll still have me."

Matt turned and extended his hand to me. I was stunned, a wave of shock roiling through my body at this recent turn of events. Jenna nudged me. She smiled and nodded, encouraging me to go to him.

"Yes, yes of course!" I ran to him. He caught me as I jumped into his arms.

"I love you, Ali-gator. I've never stopped loving you."

"I love you too, Matt."

We wrapped our arms around each other. Our lips met and an electrifying current ran through my body. It felt good. It felt right.

"I love a good love story," Marlo said.

I chuckled as I broke off the kiss. "Let's go home."

Chapter 19

A purple leather bound book rested on the desk. I ran my fingers over the cover, relishing the texture of the material. I unclasped the metal lock and opened the book to the first page. Sitting down, I grabbed a pen. It had been ages since I'd done this, but Marlo had suggested I give this a go to get my feelings out so I could move forward with my life.

Dear Diary,

It's an understatement to say the past year of my life has been interesting. It has been transformational in more ways than the obvious, but at least I now feel I have closure, or at least closure is within grasp.

It's almost Thanksgiving, and I have so much to be thankful for. I'm alive, so to speak, and with Matt, the love of my life. But let me back up a bit.

Everything, and I mean everything, has been settled with the Ruling Council. After the fiasco at Buzzard's Roost, there was a special assembly for the seated members of the Ruling Council. The Drake siblings, Zeke and myself were the only non-seated members permitted. The Council felt it necessary to limit the audience after hearing the purpose of the meeting from Lucretia. Lucious and his cronies were grilled, but when questioned, Lucious didn't offer up much about what went on while he was trapped in the Garden of Eden with Cain. Lucious claims he killed Cain, but I think he said that only to save face. At least I hope it's not the truth, and my long lost relative is residing peacefully in paradise. Lucious was found guilty of working with the enemy – gypsies – for his personal gain. Although Lucious technically didn't break one of the three existing vampire laws, the Council felt it appropriate to set a precedent. I have a feeling a new law may hit the books soon.

Caz and Delilah were found guilty of murdering Felix. Though neither would fess up to their specific role or admit who fired the shots that killed Felix, there were enough accusations to prove both of them guilty. Funny how quickly allies turn on each other when they are interrogated separately and the interrogator tells slight lies ensuring one suspect turns on the other.

Jal was found guilty of also working with the enemy—vampires. He was convicted for the crime of accessing the Garden—twice—without permission from his elders.

Vincent was found guilty of transforming me into a vampire without my consent and a laundry list of other offenses.

The punishment doled out to all of them was life in prison on Rattlesnake Island. I was somewhat shocked by the Council's leniency, but Zeke recited Felix's final request that his murderer not be killed, but locked away for an eternity of suffering. The Council saw reason in that for Lucious and company. As for Vincent, Lorenzo pointed out Vincent's falsified historical accounts and his execution would prevent us from ever knowing the truth. The Council agreed. After all, we were leaving behind those historical records for the next generation and they needed the truth on which to base their decisions.

Now that the existence and purpose of the Secret Coven was revealed to the Council, everything was out on the table. Lorenzo explained how the Coven was founded by Ina, Cain's vampire companion, for the purposes of protecting her and Cain from Lucious' vendetta, and then how the mission transformed into watching over descendants once the first was conceived and how that mission had continued over the centuries. The seated members learned about descendants like me, offspring of Cain's affair with a mortal once he was a vampire. I answered all of the Council's questions the best I could. It felt refreshing to tell the truth about who I really was. It was as if the truth had set me free.

I'm even out of hot water with the Council for Sam and Brian's murders. In the days following the great revelation, as I now refer to it, news broke that the identities of the murderers had been discovered. Tips led to Casper Devoe and Delilah Ducarme as the culprits. You could imagine my surprise when I heard this on the news. I had no idea how the police had come to that conclusion considering I was guilty of those murders. I asked Zeke about this, but he confirmed nothing. I surmised that Zeke had used his ability to transform into mist and entered the police station, altering the evidence. Zeke didn't comment; he only smiled at my theory. Whatever he did, as I'm positive he did something, I'm eternally grateful. The police will be looking for Caz and Delilah, who of course they won't find since they're incarcerated on Rattlesnake Island. Thank goodness the Ruling Council pressure is now off me.

Speaking of Zeke, I've spent a lot of time talking with him over the past weeks. I wanted to know his story and talking with him made me feel *like Felix was still present. Zeke asked a lot of questions about me, as Felix hadn't given him too much information. But I'm not sure where Zeke is now. After several heart-to-hearts, he disappeared. Wherever he is, I hope he's happy.*

As for Gabriela, Matt had heard from some of his angel buddies that she was in hot water with Saint Michael himself for her inability to properly train Matt and bring him into the fold. But she was in hotter water for what she had planned to do to me. It seems the other angels who had accompanied Gabriela to Buzzard's Roost to "permanently take care of me" turned on Gabriela under questioning. They ratted her out, confessing she was the mastermind behind the plan. After further investigation, the Army also discovered the mole—the person who had learned of the existence of the bullets that could kill a vampire, who stole the bullets and sold them to Caz and Delilah—was one of Gabriela's subordinates. It seems she is now the recipient of all that Army punishment she's been talking about.

And speaking of the Army, Matt has been dishonorably discharged. Matt's insistence that he was going to be with me led to this decision. He argued that the Army couldn't do anything about it since I was part angel. Coupled with the fact the Army permitted our marriage to happen in the first place, before Matt knew he was an angel and I knew I was a descendant, the sacred bond of marriage outweighed the angels' law about angels and vampires commingling. Matt had to swear himself to secrecy as part of the deal that he wouldn't reveal the Army or its mission to anyone.

With all of this behind me, I could finally move on. I abandoned my house in Ridge Hollow, and Matt listed our home in Buzzard Hill for sale. We found a farmhouse on fifty acres literally in the middle of nowhere—the type of home and town where Matt had always wanted to live. We have no neighbors, and the nearest town is a thirty-minute drive. It affords the tranquility I now desire.

The property is beautiful. The area around the home is filled with fruit trees and flowers and grassy fields. The leaves have turned their fall colors, but I look forward to spring and summer when I can prune the plants and harvest the fruit. There's a Willow Tree behind the home that's almost as tall as the farmhouse. It was there, under the weeping branches where Matt and I remarried. Jenna officiated. She's not ordained, but Matt and I didn't care. The act itself meant something to us.

I've never been happier. The only thing that can make me happier is living out the rest of Matt's mortal days with him. He's my soulmate, my one true love. Matt lost his immortaility after being discharged from the Army, and this is the only way we can be together forever, as the alternative—transforming Matt into a vampire—is not. Once he passes, I plan to as well.

In keeping with Felix's last words, my decision will also spare the souls of those mortals I would have killed if I were still alive. We'll be buried in our family crypt, next to my parents, as it had always been planned. This is my wish, and I will make it known by sending two separate notes: one to Jenna, and one to Marlo, to ensure this happens exactly as I intend.

A knock at the door interrupted my next thought. I paused, pen in hand, and waited, unsure if I'd actually heard a knock. Considering the remote location, I would never have expected an unannounced visitor. I heard it again.

I set the pen down and rose from the chair. I exited the spare bedroom, which functioned as a den, and crept down the hallway to our bedroom. I peeked in. Matt was still asleep, his chest rising and falling with each breath, and our new pet, Hope, a barn cat who had somehow made our house her home, slept next to him. I closed the door and walked down the stairs.

I stretched before opening the door, extending my arms high into the air and then took a sip of my coffee. The bitter brew didn't taste right and upset my stomach. I'd have to make a fresh pot after dealing with the visitor.

As the person knocked a third time, I pulled open the door.

"Lucretia?"

"Hello, Allison."

"But how did you…" And before I could finish asking my question, I realized I already knew the answer.

Lucretia smiled at my realization.

"I'm going to have to get my framed rose back from you."

"Mmm, I think I'm going to hang onto it for a bit longer."

"What do you want, Lucretia?"

"You and Matthew are back together?"

"I'm guessing you already know the answer."

"Does Matthew know about your relationship with Vincent?"

"I don't have a relationship with Vincent," I replied bluntly.

Lucretia chuckled. "Your past relationship with Vincent."

"What kind of question is that?"

"Does Matthew know you've slept with Vincent?"

I cocked my head and inhaled sharply. What business was it of hers to be asking these questions? Stepping over the threshold, I closed the door behind me without shutting it. "What do you really want, Lucretia?"

"If you haven't told Matthew yet, you may want to."

My eyes narrowed as I studied her face, trying to figure out her end game. Her eyes traveled down to my stomach and then back to my face. The corners of her mouth turned up into a devious grin. She stepped toward me, invading all concept of personal space, and placed a hand on my stomach.

"What are you doing?" I smacked her hand away.

"So it is true."

"What's true?"

Lucretia stepped back, turning away from me, her head bowed, hand on chin, appearing deep in thought.

"Lucretia?" I called out.

"I had a vision," she said as she looked at me from the bottom of the steps. "I thought it was impossible, so I had to come here and see for myself."

"See what? What are you talking about?"

"You're pregnant, Allison."

I scoffed at the absurdity. "You're insane. That's not possible. Female vampires can't conceive."

"As with everything else about you, nothing is impossible."

My mind knew this was impossible, but my body was telling me otherwise. My sense of smell had been off the past few weeks, most scents turning my stomach. Nothing tasted as good as it normally did like the coffee this morning, not even human blood. Then there was also the soreness and the increased need for rest.

"Allison?"

"Huh," I lifted my head.

"You know it's true, don't you."

I nodded. "It's Vincent's?"

"One of them is."

"One of them?"

"You're pregnant with twins. One fathered by Vincent, the other by Matthew."

"What? How is that possible?"

"Fraternal twins by two different fathers are possible. As for how you, a female vampire, got pregnant, well that's a new mystery."

I touched my stomach as if the act would make this more real for me. I was pregnant, something I had never thought would be possible. Something I had wanted for so long and had given up on when fertility doctor after fertility doctor couldn't figure out what was wrong with me. And now I was going to have two babies. One fathered by the love of my life, the other fathered by the last person I ever wanted to see again.

"So what are you going to do?"

I cleared my throat and composed myself. "What do you mean, what am I going to do? Matt and I are going to raise these children and provide them a loving home."

"Are you going to tell Matthew about the paternity?"

"I don't think it's any of your business."

"Ali," Matt called out from upstairs. "Who's here?"

I looked back at the door and then at Lucretia. "Please don't tell anyone about this. I'm finally free of Council scrutiny, and Matt is free from the Army. We won't want any attention over this."

"What's in it for me?"

"What do you want?" I asked. I heard Matt walking down the steps.

"How about I let you know when the time comes?"

I huffed. Lucretia looked past me and tilted her head as if looking for Matt to appear any moment.

"Fine, fine, just go."

She smiled. "Good luck, Allison." Lucretia turned and was out of sight in a blink of an eye.

"Hey," Matt called out as he opened the door. "Who's here?"

"No one.""I thought I heard a knock."

"You probably heard me as I set my coffee cup on the table inside." Matt yawned and stretched. "So what do you want to do today?"

I grabbed his hand. "I have something to tell you."

"You do? How about we go back to bed and you tell me later?" He pulled me close, and I felt exactly why he wanted to go back to bed.

I smiled, holding onto his waist, I pulled back. "Matt," I stared into his hazel eyes and got butterflies in my stomach, "we're going to have a baby."

He blinked and then shook his head. "What? We are? Are you serious?"

I nodded.

"How? Wait, I don't care how this is possible, this is great news!" He beamed, already a proud father.

"It's going to be double the fun."

Matt looked at me inquisitively.

"We're having twins."

"Twins? You're kidding?" He pulled me in and bear hugged me. "This is great news, Ali-gator. You've made me the happiest man alive." He kissed my temple.

A wave of guilt rippled through me at being less than honest with him about the paternity. But with Vincent locked up for life, was there any reason to tell Matt or anyone else for that matter? And what about the baby? How would it be for him or her to grow up without a biological father? Everything would be easier this way.

"We're finally going to have the family we've always wanted," he said as he hugged tighter.

"Yes we are," I confirmed. I buried my head in Matt's shoulder as I bit my tongue, a tear rolling down my cheek. "Yes we are."

Acknowledgements

Thank goodness for car pools and lunch hours because those are the two reasons this book ever got written – seriously! There are also many others I need to thank for helping me see this book into print.

Thank you to my street team. This is a small but mighty group that helps spread the word about my books. But more than that, they're the ones who gave me a kick in the arse to keep writing this story. I consider you all good friends even if we've only met on Facebook.

Thank you to fellow authors: C.R. Everett, Kim Scott, AJ Lape, JD Nelson, Aneesa Price, and Julie Cassar. You all have saved my sanity on more than one occasion on this crazy roller coaster of a ride.

Thank you to all of my beta readers. It is your sharp eyes, criticisms and compliments that help ensure the story in my head has translated to paper.

Thank you to my editor, the wonderful Jenny Bengen-Albert. I promise you I really do know the difference between 'your' and 'you're'! I couldn't do this without you. I'm always amazed at the things you catch and your ability to reword a sentence and make it exactly what I wanted but failed to get on the page.

And last but absolutely not least, a huge thank you to my hubby and mother who are both my biggest fans and cheerleaders. Thank you for listening to my rants and joyous outbursts and ramblings and for all around supporting me and my passion.

About the Author

Kelley Grealis has loved all things vampire since she was a kid. It was that fascination, combined with the need to know how the first vampire was created, that compelled her to write the type of vampire novel she had always wanted to read. She was born and raised in Cleveland, Ohio and continues to live in the area with her husband and their two fur babies. Kelley likes her cars fast and her motorcycles loud and is a craft beer snob. When she's not writing, she's working at her day job, cruising in her convertible while blasting 80's rock, or enjoying a beer at her favorite local brewery. Connect with Kelley on her website www.KelleyGrealis.com.

37993572R00135

Made in the USA
Lexington, KY
18 December 2014